Royal Icing

The Cupcake Club

Sheryl Berk and Carrie Berk

sourcebooks
jabberwocky

Copyright © 2014 by Sheryl Berk and Carrie Berk
Cover and internal design © 2014 by Sourcebooks, Inc.
Cover design by Rose Audette
Cover illustration © Kristi Valiant

Sourcebooks and the colophon are registered trademarks of Sourcebooks, Inc.

The characters and events portrayed in this book are fictitious or are used ficti-
tiously. Any similarity to real persons, living or dead, is purely coincidental and
not intended by the author.

Published by Sourcebooks Jabberwocky, an imprint of Sourcebooks, Inc.
P.O. Box 4410, Naperville, Illinois 60567-4410
(630) 961-3900
Fax: (630) 961-2168
www.jabberwockykids.com

Library of Congress Cataloging-in-Publication data is on file with the pub-
lisher.

Source of Production: Versa Press, East Peoria, Illinois, USA
Date of Production: August 2014
Run Number: 5002318

Printed and bound in the United States of America.
VP 10 9 8 7 6 5 4 3 2 1

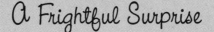

A Frightful Surprise

If there was one thing Kylie Carson enjoyed on a stormy night, it was curling up on her couch with a monster movie. Monster flicks were Kylie's favorite things in the whole world, although she couldn't exactly explain why. Most kids in fifth grade at Blakely Elementary found them creepy and weird. But Kylie insisted that all the blood, guts, and gore were good for a laugh! Plus, there was just something about a scary movie that made her happy and excited.

It felt just like when she rode a roller coaster and her stomach did a somersault as the coaster plunged down a death-defying drop. It caught her off guard and took her breath away, but afterward, she felt so *alive*. Her dad said she was a risk taker, just like her Grandpa Nathaniel, who parachuted out of airplanes when he was in the Air Force.

"Your Papa Nat was fearless," her dad explained. "He

once took your Uncle Charlie and me camping when we were kids, and a grizzly bear showed up at our tent in the middle of the night. Papa Nat didn't flinch; he stared that grizzly down!"

Kylie knew she wasn't *that* fearless. There were things that certainly scared her—like her upcoming geography test (drawing the entire world map from memory!) or forgetting a key ingredient in an important cupcake recipe.

She loved cupcakes almost as much as monsters. Back in fourth grade, she had taken a risk and started her club, Peace, Love, and Cupcakes, at Blakely, hoping it would help her fit in at her new school. Amazingly, she made three of the best friends a girl could ever ask for—Jenna, Sadie, and Lexi—and added a fourth, Delaney, when she went to summer camp.

Together, they were now so much more than an after-school club. PLC was a huge baking business, whipping up hundreds of cupcakes every month for all sorts of parties and events. No order was too big, too small, or too unusual for PLC to tackle. In fact, the stranger, the better in Kylie's book! Just last week, a woman had called requesting a dozen cupcakes for her horse's fifth birthday at the Danbury Stables. Jenna had come up with the idea to make minis out of molasses, carrot, apple, and oatmeal. They presented them to Buttercup on a horseshoe-shaped platter. Mission accomplished!

Tonight, since the forecast called for showers, Kylie decided to invite all her PLCers over for a sleepover party. She dubbed it "A Night of Fright and Frosting," and Lexi was first on her list to call.

"I'm down for the frosting part." Lexi hesitated. She was always a little timid and needed some coaxing. "It's the fright part that scares me."

"That's the point," Kylie assured her. "Monster movies are supposed to be creepy, spooky, spine-tingling…"

"Can I bring my boo-boo teddy bear?" Lexi asked.

Kylie chuckled. "Sure, if it makes you feel better. I'm thinking a double feature: *The Blob*, then *Ghost of Frankenstein*. Bela Lugosi and Boris Karloff. It doesn't get any better than that."

"Sure it does," Lexi insisted. "We could watch something fun and happy and monster-free. I could ask Delaney to bring over some of her baby brother and sister's *Sesame Street* DVDs. Come on! Aren't you just an itty-bitty bit nostalgic for Elmo?"

"Technically, Elmo is a monster," Kylie replied.

"A cute, red, fuzzy-wuzzy one!" Lexi tossed back. "With a big orange nose!"

"I think Frankenstein is cute—in a green, undead sort of way," Kylie teased. She knew scary flicks weren't exactly Lexi's thing, so she had to think fast.

"You know, I was kind of hoping you'd bring your sketchbook over and help me come up with a design for a new order: thirty dozen cupcakes for the opening of the New Fairfield Amateur Art Show."

"Art? Did you say art?" Lexi's ears perked up. Art was always up her alley! Her artistic eye and talent for painting and drawing had made her PLC's expert cupcake decorator. She dreamed of one day having an exhibit at a famous art museum—like the Met in New York City, the Louvre in Paris, or the National Gallery in London. "What kind of an art show?"

"The lady who placed the order said it's for all local artists in the Connecticut area. I was thinking maybe you'd want to create an awesome painting and enter it in the contest."

"OMG! That's amazing! I'll be right over!"

An hour later when Lexi rang her doorbell, Kylie had finished inviting over the rest of the club and was poking around in the kitchen cupboards.

"Kylie, honey, Lexi's here," her mom said, ushering Lexi into the kitchen. "And she brought her entire art studio."

Kylie looked up from the shelves of spices. Lexi had an easel under one arm and a canvas under the other.

"I didn't bring my entire studio," she corrected Mrs. Carson. "Just my oil paints, brushes, a couple of canvases in case I make a mistake…"

Kylie shook her head. "As if you ever make a mistake," she said, climbing down from her step stool. "Lex, your paintings are all masterpieces and so are your cupcakes."

"Which is why I had this great idea," Lexi said, opening her bag and pulling out her sketchbook. "Cupcakes are art—you know that and I know that. So why not prove it to everyone else?"

She held up a drawing she'd made in pastel colored pencils. It was a beautifully frosted cupcake, dotted with rainbow sprinkles.

"Everyone else will probably paint landscapes or flowers or horses. I thought a still life of a cupcake would shake things up a little."

"I think that's a brilliant idea," Kylie replied. "Maybe we should do mini versions of your painting on each cupcake. How cool would that be? If anyone can paint an awesome cupcake, it's you, Lexi."

"I agree!" said a voice outside the kitchen. It was Sadie, followed by Jenna with Delaney tagging along behind her. Sadie, as always, was on her skateboard. She was the sportiest girl in the cupcake club, but had proved she was an awesome baker as well.

"The door was open, so we came in," Jenna said. "Do I smell buttered popcorn? I'm starved!" Other kids in school teased her for being overweight, but all the PLC girls loved Jenna just the way she was.

Kylie chuckled. "How do you say it, Jenna? *Mi casa es tu casa?*"

Jenna tried to be polite. "Yeah, that's kinda how you say it…only with a much better Spanish accent."

Kylie jumped down and gathered up a pile of DVDs she'd placed on the kitchen counter. "Let's get the monster movie fest under way!"

They gathered on the rug in front of the TV, where Kylie had arranged pillows and bowls of popcorn.

"I'll sit over here." Lexi pointed to the couch. She took the throw blanket on it and wrapped it around herself. "In case I need to duck for cover."

"I don't think you'll need that," Kylie's mom said, popping a DVD into the player. "I spoke to Juliette earlier today, and she dropped off something she wants you girls to watch."

"Hey!" Kylie protested. "I have a whole lineup of monster movies planned!" It wasn't like their club advisor to spring something on them. She usually consulted Kylie first. After all, Kylie was PLC's president.

"I think you'll want to see this," her mom replied. "Especially since Juliette has a big surprise for all of you and she'll be here in an hour to tell you about it."

"A surprise?" Delaney asked. "What kind of surprise?" The last "big surprise" she had was her mom announcing she was pregnant with twins! "Monster movies don't scare me, but surprises do." Delaney was PLC's comic relief—until she became a big sister a few months ago. But no matter how "serious" and responsible she tried to be, she was always the life of the party with a flair for the dramatic.

The DVD began to play, and beautiful pink posies appeared on the screen. Then yellow daisies, then white chrysanthemums. There was sweeping music, and the words "My Fair Lady" and a list of names materialized.

"This doesn't look like *The Blob*." Kylie sighed.

Lexi leaned in for a closer look. "No! It's beautiful!"

Sadie giggled. "But Kylie thinks *The Blob* is beautiful."

"You bet I do," Kylie grumped.

"In a red, ooey-gooey kinda way," Delaney said.

"Watching *The Blob* always kind of makes me hungry for Jell-O," Jenna added. "With whipped cream and bananas."

"Guys! Can we please focus on the movie!" Lexi insisted. "What do you think Juliette's surprise is? Do you think it has to do with flowers? Maybe we're doing cupcakes for the New York Botanical Garden!"

Just then, a figure appeared on-screen. He was a proper English gentleman with a proper English accent. He wore a tweed hat and a trench coat, and was making quite a fuss over the way a girl selling flowers was speaking.

"I think my sister did this musical in tenth grade," Jenna said. "This guy is gonna teach her how to be a lady."

"It's based on a famous play by George Bernard Shaw called *Pygmalion*," Mrs. Carson explained.

Kylie wrinkled her nose. "Who would name their play *Pig-Mail*? Pigs play in the mud. They don't deliver mail."

Her mom giggled. "*Pygmalion*. It has nothing to do with pigs, and it's a classic. But I'll let Juliette explain the significance when she gets here."

All the girls were enthralled with the movie—all except Kylie. The man on the screen was complaining, "Why can't the English teach their children how to speak?" He looked angry and frustrated, and she knew just how he felt.

Why couldn't her cupcake club simply watch a monster movie?

2

Juliette's Big News

By the time their club advisor arrived, they had reached the part in the movie where Eliza Doolittle, the flower girl, and Henry Higgins, the language teacher, were waltzing around his study singing "The Rain in Spain."

"This is the best movie I've ever seen," Lexi exclaimed.

"I know!" Delaney chimed in, jumping on the couch and singing along. "Who knew the rain in Spain stays mainly in the plain?"

"I'm so glad you feel that way," Juliette said, taking off her coat. "It's pretty magical, isn't it?"

Kylie rolled her eyes. "I don't get what's so great about it. He teaches her how to pronounce her words with some silly rain-plain-Spain tongue twister. Big deal. It's not like he killed any vampires or zombies!"

Juliette chuckled. "I don't think Henry Higgins

would make a very good vampire slayer," she told Kylie. "I suppose Rodney will be relieved to hear that."

Kylie wondered why Juliette's fiancé would even care—aside from the fact that his last name was Higgins too. Mr. Higgins was always swept up in teaching Shakespeare to kids at Blakely Elementary. He was a trained actor, just like Juliette, and he loved catching his audience off guard. He had, after all, planted Juliette's engagement ring in a cupcake! Maybe he was behind all this. "Does this have to do with your surprise?" she asked Juliette.

"It does." Juliette paused the DVD and cleared her throat. "Rodney is going to be playing Henry Higgins in a new revival of *Pygmalion* in the West End."

"Awesome!" Delaney cheered. "Can we go see his opening night in the city? I've always wanted to walk the red carpet."

"The West End isn't in New York City," Juliette explained. "It's in London."

"London, as in England?" Jenna gasped.

"Yes, London, England," their advisor replied. "And opening night happens to be during your spring break. Which means it's the perfect time for you to come with me. I spoke to all of your parents and asked their permission for PLC to cater cupcakes for the opening-night party. Everyone said yes."

"We're going to London!" Lexi squealed as she jumped up and down on the couch. Kylie had never seen her so excited.

Juliette nodded. "If it's okay with all of you."

"Okay? It's amazing!" Delaney cheered. "Do you think we can meet the Queen?"

"I've always wanted to check out a football game in England—that's what they call soccer over there," Sadie said. "Do you think we can find a match?"

"I've heard the Queen has Prestat chocolates delivered to Buckingham Palace," Jenna added. "I've been dying to try their red velvet truffles!"

Kylie was quiet as the rest of the girls chattered away about the trip.

"Is there a problem, Kylie?" Juliette asked her. "You don't seem excited."

"I think it's great that Rodney is starring in a play and that you asked us to go with you," Kylie said.

"Then what's wrong?" Juliette asked. "I thought you of all people would be doing the happy dance."

Kylie shrugged. "It's just that we usually talk about our orders ahead of time and vote on any big decisions."

Juliette nodded. "You're right, Kylie. I should have

consulted you first. We should consider it carefully and put it to a vote. It will be a lot of work: the producers of the show want two hundred cupcakes for opening night and a fun display."

"Kyles, are you crazy?" Delaney said, shaking Kylie by the shoulders. "This is awesome. We're going to London! We're going to an opening-night party filled with all sorts of celebrities. OMG! What if One Direction comes?"

Juliette reached into her purse and pulled out a pamphlet that the travel agent had given her. "I thought this might be of some interest to you, Kylie," she said, handing it to her. It read "The London Tombs."

Kylie's eyes grew wide. "Tombs? Real tombs?"

"I understand you walk through the plague pits," Juliette said. "And there's a London ghost tour, and an amazing monster exhibit at Madame Tussauds wax museum." She pulled out several more brochures. "Plus London has lots of wonderful cupcakes to sample. Rodney tells me the Harrods Food Halls are just filled with them."

Juliette had just said the two magic words: "monster" and "cupcake." Still Kylie hesitated. No matter how great the trip sounded, it felt a little like she was losing control of her club. All the girls were swarming around Juliette, pressing her for details of the trip. They hadn't even asked Kylie *her* opinion.

Before she could say another word, Juliette called for a vote: "All in favor of a PLC going to London say, 'Cupcake!'"

"Cupcake!" Jenna, Sadie, Lexi, and Delaney all shouted in unison.

Kylie forced a smile and tried to remind herself of all the great things the trip had to offer—even if it hadn't been her idea in the first place.

3

I Dream of London

Two days later, Kylie called an official meeting of PLC to discuss their next few months of business. "Shall we get started?" Juliette asked her, glancing at the clock. "Mrs. Rogner and the math team need the teachers' lounge at four forty-five…"

"Yeah, and I've got b-ball practice at four thirty," Sadie added.

"Oh! I have a science test to study for," Lexi said. "The food chain isn't my strongest topic."

"A chain of food sounds pretty awesome to me," Jenna said. "I'm starving. Anybody bring a snack?" She looked through the bag of groceries Kylie had brought and found a bag of mini bittersweet chocolate chips.

"That's our stock for our weekend bake," Delaney reminded her.

"I'm the official taste tester. So I'm tasting!" Jenna said with a wink.

Kylie looked annoyed. No one was listening to her. They were too busy chattering and passing around the bag of chocolate chips. She cleared her throat and tapped a wooden spoon on the kitchen countertop. Everyone grew silent.

"I hereby call this meeting of Peace, Love, and Cupcakes to order," she announced.

Most of what they needed to discuss was business as usual: a dozen cupcakes for a seventh birthday party Thursday, and a dozen more for an anniversary dinner Friday night.

"I think we should divide and conquer," Kylie suggested. "Jenna and Lexi, you come to my house tomorrow and we'll do the birthday boy's NASCAR-themed cupcakes, and Laney and Sadie, you guys handle the anniversary couple's double mocha fudge chip."

Lexi cut her off: "Can we talk about the design of the opening-night *Pygmalion* cupcakes?" She pulled out her sketchbook and passed it around the group. "I've been working on it since your monster-movie sleepover, and I really think this is it."

Delaney turned the notebook upside down, then right side up. "I don't get it," she said. "It's an umbrella, a floppy hat, and an airplane."

"That floppy hat is a sombrero," Jenna corrected her. "It's a Mexican hat. But Delaney's right, Lex. I don't get it either."

Lexi snapped her fingers in the air. "The rain in Spain stays mainly in the plane! Remember? It's the best song in the whole movie!"

Juliette chuckled. "It's the *plain*—as in a flat land. Not an airplane, Lexi. It's not really supposed to make sense. It's a speech exercise."

"Oh," Lexi said, blushing. "I thought it was kinda strange that it would rain inside an airplane…but it looks so good in the sketch!"

"It does!" Delaney nodded. "I like Lexi's version better."

"We have plenty of time to talk about London." Kylie tried to steer them back to the pressing business at hand. "The trip's not for three weeks."

"I know! But it's so exciting!" Lexi said. "Who can think about race car cupcakes when we're about to see Big Ben and the London Bridge up close and personal?"

"I had this dream last night," Sadie interjected. "I was kicking around a soccer ball with David Beckham, and he told me that since he'd retired, he needed someone to take his place. So I became a champion English footballer!"

Kylie sighed. "Can we please focus?"

"Do you know," added Jenna, "that Banoffee Pie is an English dessert made with bananas, cream, and toffee? How cool is that?"

Kylie looked at Delaney. "Aren't you going to say something about London too?" Delaney just stared, glassy eyed.

"Hello? Earth to Delaney?" Kylie said, poking her.

"Oh! Sorry! I was just imagining myself arm in arm with Daniel Radcliffe at the *Pygmalion* opening-night party. Do you think I should wear my Hogwarts scarf—or is that too much?"

Juliette smiled. "I'm really glad you girls are so excited about the trip," she said. "And I don't think it hurts to plan ahead. Do you, Kylie?"

Kylie shrugged. "I guess."

"I like where Lexi was going with the *My Fair Lady* cupcake idea," Juliette added. "What else from the movie inspires us?"

"Flowers!" Delaney suddenly shouted. "What if we make the cupcakes in flower flavors?"

Sadie looked puzzled. "Are you supposed to eat flowers? I thought you just looked at them and smelled them."

"Nuh-uh," Jenna insisted. "I saw an episode of *Battle of*

the Bakers where the contestants had to do cupcakes for the Tournament of Roses parade. All the flavors were flowery, like hibiscus and orange blossom."

Kylie tried once more to take charge. "Maybe we should do some research first and regroup another day for a taste test. In the meantime, there's the order for the Amateur Art Show that we still need to discuss."

"OMG! The art show!" Lexi cried. She'd almost forgotten they had an order for thirty dozen cupcakes due this weekend, not to mention her art entry.

"I'm almost finished with my painting, so all that's left is to make a mini version on the cupcakes," she said.

Delaney scratched her head. "You're gonna paint cupcakes?"

"Kinda," Lexi replied. "I thought we could paint little fondant canvases with food coloring and frame them with a gold border."

Jenna smacked her lips together. "Talk to me about flavors."

"We need to think artsy and colorful," Lexi replied.

"How about vanilla rainbow tie-dye cupcakes?" Kylie asked. "That's as colorful as it gets." She flipped through her binder of recipes. "I've always wanted to try this. Basically, once you make the batter, you divide it into smaller bowls and dye each one a different color—red, yellow, blue, green, purple. Then you drizzle the different colors into each cupcake liner and give 'em a swirl with a toothpick."

Jenna studied the recipe closely. "With all this color going on, the frosting has to look clean and simple but taste delicious. How about a white fluffy marshmallow buttercream?"

"Love it," Kylie replied. "I think we've got a plan."

☆ ☮ ☆

When they met to bake the order two days later, Lexi came prepared. "I wanted to get us all in the mood for our assignment today," she said, digging into her tote bag. She pulled out five tie-dyed aprons. "I did them myself. Cool, huh?"

"Amazing!" Delaney said, tying one around her waist.

"These are great," Sadie added. "My old apron was getting really tired."

"It's very pretty, Lexi," Kylie told her. "It's just not our 'official' PLC apron."

"Yeah? So?" Lexi said. "Everything doesn't have to be so 'by the books,' Kylie."

Kylie took a deep breath. "It does! That's how baking cupcakes works," she insisted. "You follow the recipe word for word, or something is bound to go wrong. Do you remember the time Sadie accidentally swapped strawberry syrup for strawberry preserves in our shortcake cupcakes?"

Sadie shook her head. "Yeah, that was a disaster. Those cupcakes came out like soup. My bad!"

"Which is exactly why we have to always go by the book," Kylie added.

"I think it's fun to push the envelope," Lexi insisted. "Great artists always try new things."

"Our tie-dye cupcake recipe is new," Kylie pointed out. But she was getting nowhere. All the girls loved their new aprons. She put on her old purple PLC one, like the others she'd made for the club when they first went into business. It was covered with stains and fraying at the edges, but it had a lot of great memories.

"Whatever," she shrugged, and gathered ingredients. "Jenna, what kind of vanilla are we using?"

"That was a tough one," Jenna replied. "I was torn between my two favorites, Mexican and Tahitian."

"And?" Sadie asked. "What's the verdict?"

"Neither! Let's mix it up this time and go for this!"

She held up a bottle labeled "Genuine Hawaiian Vanilla Extract."

"Cool!" Delaney said. "Does it taste different?"

Jenna put a tiny amount on her fingertip. "A little. It's sweeter and has a really nice aroma."

She held the bottle under Kylie's nose. "Don't ya think?"

Kylie took a sniff. "I guess. Are you sure you don't want to use our usual vanilla? I mean our vanilla cupcakes are delicious. Why tamper with perfection?"

"I dunno. I thought it would be fun to try something a little different," Jenna replied. "Like Lexi said, we should push the envelope."

"The envelope doesn't need pushing! It's fine where it is!" Kylie shouted.

"Kylie, are you okay?" Delaney asked her gently. "We're just trying to have some fun."

"Yeah, you seem a little stressed," Jenna added. "Ever since Juliette mentioned the London trip, you've been kinda grumpy."

"I'm not grumpy about London. Or the new aprons. Or the new vanilla. Or changing my monster movie night into watching a musical. I just feel like you guys don't need me anymore!" Kylie blurted out.

"That's loco, *chica*!" Jenna said, putting her arm around her friend. "You're our club president and BFF. Of course we need you!"

"Why? You obviously don't need me to help you make decisions for PLC!" She stormed out of the teachers' lounge kitchen, slamming the door behind her. She knew she was overreacting—the girls and Juliette all meant well—but she couldn't help it. She felt like PLC was slipping through her fingertips and she was helpless to stop it.

4

Heart to Heart

Kylie's mom knocked gently on her bedroom door.

"You okay, honey? Wanna talk about it?"

Kylie buried her head in her cupcake pillow—the one Lexi had given her for her last birthday. "No."

"Sometimes it makes you feel better if you talk about what's bothering you. Maybe I can help." Mrs. Carson pushed the door open a crack. "Can I try?"

"Fine!" Kylie said, rolling over. "But I don't think you can."

"What's up?" her mom said, sitting on the edge of the bed. "Does it have to do with school? Boys? Friends?"

"It's just that everything is changing, Mom. The girls. The cupcake club."

"How?" her mom asked. "You guys haven't stopped baking cupcakes, right? It's not Peace, Love, and Pancakes now, is it?"

"No. It's just that they don't need me anymore."

"Aha," her mother said. "You mean everyone has become really smart, mature, and independent. They can think for themselves and do things without any help."

"Exactly! It's so annoying!" Kylie said, yanking the pillow over her head.

"Interesting. I know just what that feels like."

Kylie peeked out. "You do?"

"Absolutely. It was only a few short years ago that a girl I knew couldn't braid her own hair, tie her shoes, make her bed…"

"Mom," Kylie groaned. "It's not the same as me growing up and doing those things."

"Isn't it?" her mom insisted. "It makes me sad and a little scared that you don't need me as much as you used to. But it also makes me proud. It tells me I'm doing something right because you're learning to stand on your own two feet."

Kylie sat up. "Really? You feel that way sometimes?"

"All the time. More and more every day. Especially the proud part."

"So you think I should just roll with it. Not get upset if my friends leave me in the dust?"

"Honey," her mom said, stroking her hair. "They're not leaving you in the dust. You're right there with them.

You just need to understand that people grow and things change. It's part of life. That doesn't mean that the girls love you any less." She planted a kiss on Kylie's forehead and got up and walked to the door.

"Mommy?" Kylie called after her. "Thanks."

☆ ☮ ☆

On Saturday morning, Kylie got up early and biked to the New Fairfield Amateur Art Show. Her friends were already there when she arrived, unloading the cupcakes and Lexi's painting from Sadie's dad's contracting truck.

Lexi's face lit up when she saw her. "Kylie! You came!"

"Are you kidding? I wouldn't miss it for the world," Kylie said. "And I'm sorry I bailed on you guys the other day. I shouldn't have left you to bake all those cupcakes."

"That was not cool, *chica*." Jenna pouted. "We were up to our elbows in rainbow-colored batter."

"I'm really sorry," Kylie pleaded with her. "It won't happen again, I promise."

"Okay, we forgive you," Jenna said, hugging her. "As long as you mean that. We stick together, remember?"

"Like Delaney's marshmallow buttercream frosting." Sadie chuckled. "It was so gooey, my fingers were glued together!"

"That was just the first batch," Delaney pointed out. "I overdid it on the Marshmallow Fluff. It happens…"

"Where should we put this masterpiece?" Sadie's dad asked, lifting out Lexi's huge cupcake canvas. It was so detailed—with mountains of whipped pink frosting and glittery sprinkles—that it looked good enough to eat.

"Over there." Lexi pointed to an open easel in the center of the showroom. The gallery was filled with artwork, everything from paintings and charcoal drawings to a giant sculpture made out of old soda cans and license plates.

"What is that?" Sadie asked. "It looks like a pile of junk."

Lexi shook her head. "That's not junk. It's someone's entry. Art is in the eye of the beholder."

"I get that," Sadie answered. "But I could probably make something like that out of the garbage we have in our garage."

"Hey!" her dad protested. "Are you calling my record collection garbage?"

Sadie rolled her eyes. "Dad, no one listens to Spyro Gyra anymore!"

"I've never even heard of him—or her—or them before," Delaney said.

"What? 'Morning Dance' is a classic!" Mr. Harris replied. "You girls don't know what you're missing."

"Speaking of art, where do we put our cupcakes?" Jenna asked. "Do you see anybody in charge around here?" They scanned the room, but everyone was busy unpacking and setting up.

Lexi pointed to a corner where there was an open table draped with a white cloth. "I think the cupcakes are supposed to go there," she said.

Kylie helped carry them in and set them out on display. It was Lexi's idea to place them on a blank canvas. "They are so beautiful, guys," she said. "And Jenna you were totally right. That Hawaiian vanilla smells amazing."

"*Por supuesto!* Of course it does!"

"Ladies and gentleman…" A voice suddenly boomed over a loudspeaker. "If we can have all of our artists please stand by their work, the judging is about to start."

Kylie gave Lexi a gentle push. "Go get 'em, Lex. We'll be right here if you need us." She, Jenna, Sadie, and Delaney took their places behind the cupcake table.

It took the panel of three judges more than an hour to make their way around the crowded room. There were artists of all ages—from kids to grandparents. One older lady in a wheelchair proudly showed off her papier-mâché sculpture.

"It's my Peekapoo puppy, Scooty," she said. "Isn't it lifelike?"

The judges looked closely, admiring how she had etched tiny lines to represent fur in the plaster. "Quite detailed," said one of the judges, a gray-haired gentleman with a mustache. "I can see how much work you put into it." The woman beamed.

When they arrived at Lexi's painting, the judges stared long and hard for several minutes.

"What do you call it?" one judge asked her.

"Sweet Sensation," Lexi replied proudly.

"I see," he answered.

Lexi gulped. He wasn't smiling. None of the judges were. In fact, the one with short black hair and an earring in her nose looked bored.

"I've seen so many still lifes today." She yawned. "You've seen one, you've seen them all."

"It's a cupcake—it's very different from a bowl of apples," Lexi tried to explain. "And if you look over there, my friends and I did all the cupcakes for the art show with a mini painting on them. Because cupcakes are truly art."

The other female judge with bright red hair turned to see where Lexi was pointing. "Oh, my! Isn't that interesting!"

All three judges made their way to the cupcake table. "Have one? Or two or three!" Kylie said, offering them each a treat. "This was all Lexi's idea. Amazing, huh?"

The redheaded judge took a bite. "Heavens! So many colors!"

"I know! Cool, isn't it?" Kylie said, offering her a second. "It's a rainbow tie-dye cupcake."

"Spectacular use of primary shades," the gentleman added, licking frosting off his upper lip.

"It's rad," the third judge decreed.

"Is rad bad...or good?" Delaney whispered to Kylie.

"I don't know. But I think we're about to find out." The judges huddled and began to debate the entries.

"They hated it." Lexi sighed, joining her fellow PLCers. "I think I put one of them to sleep."

"Come on, Lex. Don't give up yet!" Kylie said, squeezing her friend's hand. "You did an amazing job. Let's wait and see what they say."

After much deliberation, the judges handed an envelope to a woman in a pink suit at the back of the room. The lady smiled and stepped up to the microphone.

"Hello, everyone," she said cheerfully. "My name is Meghan Wilkie, and I am the president of the New Fairfield Amateur Art Society. Welcome to our fifth annual spring show." The crowd applauded—all except for Lexi, who was biting her nails.

"I am so pleased to see such a wonderful turnout this morning, and such a wide array of artwork. Everything from paintings, sculptures, and videos to art of the edible variety." She motioned to the cupcake table.

"Did she just call our cupcakes art?" Jenna whispered.

"So now, without any further ado, I would like to announce third place. It goes to Neal Dutta for his amazing recyclable art installation entitled 'Scrap Heap!'"

The crowd cheered as Sadie watched the artist come up and claim his white ribbon. "That junk won? That is nuts!" she said.

"Shhh!" Lexi hushed her. She was now pacing the floor. "I can't take the suspense!"

"In second place, we have 'Pears on a Platter' by Charity Jackson. Congratulations!" A teenage girl with wavy brown hair stepped up to receive her red ribbon.

"Oh, no! Another still life won? I'll never win now!" Lexi said, burying her head in Kylie's shoulder.

"And finally, I'm proud to bestow first place on a most unusual artistic display," Mrs. Wilkie continued. "The judges were unanimous that this one deserved the top prize today."

"Just say it already!" Jenna exclaimed. "*Quien ganó?* Who won?"

Mrs. Wilkie smiled. "Very well. Congratulations, Lexi Poole and Peace, Love, and Cupcakes, for your Rainbow Tie-Dye Cupcakes!"

Kylie grabbed Lexi and shook her. "You won! You won!"

"We won!" Lexi shouted, jumping up and down. She pulled Kylie up to the podium with her to receive the award.

"When I ordered cupcakes for our party, I never expected you to create a work of art that would take first prize," Mrs. Wilkie told them. "Great job, ladies."

The girls celebrated as everyone at the art show gobbled up every last rainbow-colored crumb.

"I feel bad. I don't deserve this. You all do," Kylie told her club mates. "I bailed on you."

"Are you kidding? You were the one who came up with the tie-dye recipe," Lexi insisted. "You were the one who encouraged me to do mini paintings on the cupcakes."

"It was a team effort," Sadie chimed in. "Kylie, we could never have won without you."

For the first time in the past few days, Kylie actually felt needed. Maybe her mom was right. Change wasn't always a bad thing.

5

A Rose by Any Other Name

With the art show behind them, it was time to focus on the cupcakes for *Pygmalion*'s opening night. Since the club had decided on a flowery flavor, Kylie combed the Internet and her collection of cookbooks for recipes. She settled on two, then asked her mom to drive her to the baking store for the ingredients.

When PLC met at her house the next night, she produced a bottle with a pretty pink label. She cracked open the cap and waved it under Jenna's nose.

"It definitely smells rosy," Jenna said, then took a tiny taste of the clear liquid on her tongue.

"Well?" Kylie asked anxiously.

"It kind of reminds me of my *abuela*'s bath soap," Jenna replied. She wrinkled her nose. "I just don't think I'd wanna eat a whole cupcake that tastes like this."

Delaney sampled a tiny drop as well. "Eww. Now

you've gotten me picturing my mouth being washed out with soap!"

Kylie was frustrated but not ready to give up. "Okay, here's Option 2." She produced a small plastic bag filled with tiny dried purple leaves.

"What is that?" Sadie asked, "Potpourri? I think my mom keeps some of that stuff in her sock drawer."

"It's dried lavender. I got it in the spice store. I thought we could sprinkle it into the batter and frosting."

Jenna sampled a few flakes. "Maybe with honey. Something sweet to play down the floweriness?"

Sadie scratched her head. "Is 'floweriness' even a word?"

Jenna shrugged. "*No lo sé.* Beats me. But I think it might work."

"There's only one way to find out," Kylie said, handing her an apron. "Let's get baking."

Jenna decided that the first batch they took out of the oven was "too blah," while the second was so lavender scented that it made her eyes water. The third was soggy; the fourth was burnt; the fifth was chewy; and the sixth had so much lavender it stuck in Jenna's teeth. It was Lexi's idea to add food coloring to the seventh batch so the cupcakes were a lavender hue.

"You call that purple?" Sadie said, examining the gray-brown color as it came out of the oven. "It looks like mud."

"Maybe we need a few more drops of pink…or blue?" Lexi considered. "Let's do another round."

"I never thought I'd say this, but I can't taste another cupcake," Jenna announced. "*Tener compasión!* My taste buds are exhausted."

"Jenna, focus," Kylie pleaded with her. "We have to find a lavender-to-cupcake ratio that works."

"Yeah, like Goldilocks," Sadie teased. "One's not enough, one's too much, and the next one with be *just right*."

Jenna waited patiently to sample the eighth batch. She nibbled the cupcake first, then the honey cream cheese frosting, then a bite of both together. Her eyes lit up.

"Well?" Kylie asked anxiously. "Is it good?"

"*Asombroso!*" Jenna said.

Delaney elbowed Kylie. "Is that good or bad?"

"It means it's amazing," Jenna said, licking her fingers. "One of the best cupcakes we've ever made."

Kylie grabbed another cupcake off the platter and took a big bite. "It's light and delicate with just a hint of lavender. The frosting is creamy, the color of the cake is beautiful, and we sprinkled just the right amount of dried lavender on top for garnish. OMG, guys! This is perfect. We did it!"

"Do you think the actors will like it?" Sadie asked. "I hear theater people can be kinda picky."

"They'll love it when they see our amazing display," Lexi insisted. She unrolled a large sheet of paper containing her sketches. "I thought we'd get a bunch of flower baskets and fill them with cupcakes piped to look like different flowers— roses, daisies, carnations, chrysanthemums. We could dress like flower peddlers and hand them out to everyone."

"Just like Eliza Doolittle," Delaney added. "But our flowers will be a lot tastier."

"I love that idea!" Kylie exclaimed. "There's only one more thing for us to do."

Jenna rolled her eyes. "Oh, no. What's that?"

"Start packing for London!"

☆ ☮ ☆

Kylie felt like her head was swimming! There were so many details to organize. She made a long list of all the ingredients they would need and emailed it to Mr. Higgins. He'd arranged for them to use a kitchen in the culinary school that was just steps away from the theater.

"I feel like I'm forgetting something important," Kylie told her mom. "We have all the equipment and ingredients set up. What else will I need in London?"

Mrs. Carson peered into Kylie's suitcase filled with cookbooks, cupcake liners, and several of her favorite spatulas and whisks. "Are you planning on attending opening night in your PLC apron?" She chuckled. "I don't see any clothes in here."

"Oh, yeah! That!" Kylie said. She quickly rummaged through her closet and tossed several outfits in the bag. "Thanks, Mom."

"Any time." Her mom winked and handed her a pair of socks out of her drawer. "That's what moms are for."

Kylie had to admit she was actually getting excited about the trip. It was her first time in Europe. The farthest her family had ever traveled out of the United States on vacation was a long road trip to Montreal when she was eight years old. This was better because so many of her favorite monster flicks took place on the streets of London.

"Do you think I'll get to see the streets that Dr. Jekyll and Mr. Hyde walked?" she asked. "And do you know they say the London Tube is haunted by a screaming specter?"

"I certainly hope you're not going to go ghost-hunting

or wandering down any dark alleys looking for mad scientists with split personalities!" her mom teased. She made sure Kylie had her passport tucked away in her backpack and gave her some last-minute instructions.

"Make sure you stay with Juliette at all times," she cautioned Kylie. "Look both ways when crossing the street, and don't talk to strangers. Oh, and wear your retainer every night!"

"I'll be fine," Kylie assured her. It was pretty much the same speech she'd gotten when she went to Las Vegas last year for Jenna's mom's wedding. "I promise."

She saw there were tears in her mom's eyes. "Is this one of those scary, sad moments when you're also proud I'm growing up?" Kylie asked, hugging her.

"Yup," her mom replied. "I told you: I have them too."

"You'll be fine," she told her mother. "We both will."

6

Across the Pond

When the flight landed at Heathrow Airport, Delaney could barely stay in her seat until the pilot turned off the seat-belt sign. She practically leaped over Kylie to grab her bag and get off the plane.

"I've never been anywhere out of the country before," she told the airline attendant opening the overhead bins. "Do they have horses and carriages? Chimney sweeps?"

"I think you'll find London is a lot like any major city," the attendant assured her. "And there are most definitely cars."

"You've been watching way too much *Mary Poppins*," Jenna told her friend. She and Sadie were seated behind her and Kylie. "Chill, girl."

"It's just so awesome. I mean, 'ace.' That's how Londoners say it." Delaney held up a small book titled *The Best of British Slang*.

"Seriously? You're studying the native language?" Sadie asked.

"I fancy trying to fit in at the opening-night do," she said. "And there's no need to be so cheeky about it."

"You sound silly." Lexi giggled. She and Juliette had napped most of the flight. "I doubt that's how people really talk in London."

"It sure is, mate," Delaney replied. "How's about we go get us some grub? Bangers and mash? Toad in a hole? A spot of tea?"

"This is worse than my Spanish class," Sadie said. "I don't understand a thing she's saying! I'm gonna be totally lost here."

"I'm already lost." Juliette sighed as they left the plane and headed into the airport terminal. There were five terminals and a train that ran between them. "Do you suppose we go right or left?" A large sign read, "Terminal B," which is where she supposed they were. She was trying to keep track of all the girls and their carry-on bags, and find the way to baggage claim.

"Jenna! We'll have plenty of time to buy souvenirs later!" she called as Jenna made a beeline for a newsstand.

"Have you ever seen so many cool candies?" she asked

her fellow cupcakers. "*Dios mío!* This one's flakey and this one has bubbles!" She held up two colorfully wrapped chocolate bars, one that read "Flake" and another that read "Aero."

"Please, Jenna," Juliette pleaded with her. "Leave the candy, and let's try and figure out where we're going."

It took nearly an hour to go through immigration and retrieve all their bags off the luggage carousel. Juliette was counting them for the third time. "One, two, three, four…"

"Might I be of some service, madame?" a voice sang out behind them.

"Rodney!" Juliette exclaimed, dropping her luggage and racing to give her fiancé a hug and a kiss.

"Eww, gross," Delaney said, watching the pair smooch. "I mean, 'That's grotty!'"

"We're so excited for your big opening night," Kylie added.

"I'm excited you're all here," Mr. Higgins replied. "Allow me to escort you."

"My hero," Juliette said.

After they retrieved their luggage, he walked them outside to a taxi stand and held open the door of a cab. "Your chariot awaits," he said, ushering the girls inside.

Delaney looked curiously at the car. It seemed like an ordinary black cab. "What chariot? I don't see any horses."

"And how come his steering wheel is on the left side of the car?" Sadie asked, piling in. "That's weird."

"Because in London we drive on the left side of the street instead of the right," Rodney explained. "I know it's quite backwards for you but it's normal for us."

"I think you'll find many things are different and many other things are the same here," Juliette told the club. "That's the fun of exploring a new city."

"Sit back, enjoy the sights, and I'll see you later at the hotel," Rodney told her, slamming the car door closed. "I've got rehearsal till three."

"Perfect! We'll meet at the hotel for tea," Juliette replied. "I'm sure the girls would love to see what a proper afternoon tea is like."

☆ ☮ ☆

The girls had never seen a hotel as elegant and ornate as the Convoy. "Do you think that's real gold all over the ceiling?" Sadie asked as they walked into the lobby. There were several twinkly crystal chandeliers suspended from above.

"Never mind the ceiling! Have you checked out the

furniture?" Kylie asked, flopping into a red velvet chair. "I feel like I'm sitting on a throne."

"It's quite posh," Delaney agreed. "That means fancy."

"There's fancy, and then there's *fancy*," Juliette exclaimed. "How wonderful of Rodney to treat us to a suite here."

"Welcome to the Convoy," a concierge greeted them. "If there is anything I can do to make your stay more comfortable..."

Jenna tapped the gentleman on the shoulder. "Can you put some of those little chocolates on my pillow at night?"

"We have a sweets shop down the block," he replied with a wink. "I'll see what I can do."

"Okay, PLC, let's freshen up and unpack," Juliette called out.

"Did you say 'PLC'?" the concierge asked.

"Yup, that's us," Kylie replied. "You've heard of us here in England?"

The concierge pulled a large envelope from his desk and handed it to Kylie.

"For you, miss," he said. "It was just delivered."

Juliette raised an eyebrow. "Are you sure? Kylie, who would send you a letter all the way here in London?"

Kylie held the large cream-colored envelope up toward one of the chandeliers, trying to see inside. "I have no idea."

Sadie peered over her shoulder. "It looks official," she said. There was a gold wax seal on the back, stamped with some sort of coat of arms. And it was addressed in swirly calligraphy script to "PLC."

"OMG, do you think it's from Buckingham Palace?" Lexi asked. "That would be so…how do they say 'awesome' again here in London?"

"Brill!" Delaney exclaimed. "As in brilliant."

"Right! That would be brill!" Lexi replied. "Maybe Prince William and Princess Kate need some cupcakes. Or maybe the Queen has a craving for our *royal* icing!"

Jenna shook her head. "All the way here in England? *No es posible!*"

Kylie smiled. "If there's one thing I've learned after all our cupcake adventures so far, it's that *anything* is possible!"

7

Cordially Invited

Kylie took a deep breath before tearing into the envelope and pulling out the card inside.

"What does it say?" Lexi asked excitedly. "Is it from the Queen?"

"Or Prince Wills?" Sadie asked. "Maybe he needs cupcakes for his polo match."

Kylie wasn't listening. She was too engrossed in the letter.

"Kylie, we're dying of suspense," Delaney pleaded with her. "Who's it from? What does it say?"

Kylie cleared her throat and read aloud in her most proper British accent:

"The honour of your presence is hereby requested at a birthday party hosted by Lord and Lady Wakefield of Wilshire."

Jenna grabbed the card out of her hand. "It's gotta be a practical joke. Someone's pulling our leg."

Juliette nodded. "I'm afraid I've never hear of a Lord or Lady Wakefield," she said. "Maybe it was meant for someone else."

"I assure you it was intended for you," said a man sitting on a sofa in the lobby. He was tall and wearing a long black coat. "I am the attaché to Lord Wakefield."

"What's an attaché?" Delaney whispered.

Kylie shrugged. "I thought it was a briefcase my dad carried to work."

"Archibald Thomas Watson, at your service," he said, formally extending his hand to Kylie. "I believe you call it a personal assistant in the States?"

"Oh, yeah!" Delaney interrupted. "All the celebs have personal assistants. The Lord and Lady must be VIPs."

"Indeed," he replied. "And they are planning a very important party that they would like you to bake for. You come highly recommended."

Juliette was suspicious. "Really? By whom? We don't know anyone here in London."

"Oh, but you do," he insisted. "You see, my mate from university told me all about you."

Juliette's eyes grew wide. "Wait a minute…Are you… *Archie*?"

The man bowed deeply. "None other."

Juliette threw her arms around him. "It's so wonderful to finally meet you! Rodney said you'd be coming!"

"Okay…you lost me." Jenna sighed. "Who's Archie, and why is Juliette hugging him?"

"Girls, I'd like you to meet Rodney's college BFF, Archie," Juliette said, smiling. "Oh, I've heard so much about you!"

Archie blushed. "Only good things, I hope. Rodney didn't tell you the fish-and-chips story, did he? I swear, I didn't mean to get one stuck in his ear. It was all in good fun!"

Suddenly the pieces started to come together. Rodney had recommended them!

"Excuse me?" Kylie said, raising her hand. "It's very nice to meet you, Archie. But you still haven't told us what you want PLC to do."

"Of course." Archie smiled. "His Lordship is throwing a tenth birthday party this Thursday for his daughter and would like you to bake cupcakes for it. Since today's only Tuesday, I assume it's not a problem."

Kylie pulled her notebook out of her backpack. It wasn't

like PLC to turn down business, but there was so much they wanted to see and do—not to mention opening night for *Pygmalion* on Sunday.

"Let's see," she said, making some notes. "How many cupcakes are we talking?"

Archie shuffled his feet. "Oh, not all that many. Two thousand…"

Kylie gasped. "Two thousand? How many kids are coming to this party?"

"Oh, it's not just a children's party," Archie explained. "It's quite a large gathering of family, business associates, and fellow noblemen near the Tower of London."

Well, Kylie, thought, the Tower was after all at the top of their sightseeing list… Maybe they could squeeze in the cupcake order.

"Kylie," Jenna reminded her. "We said we were going to the Harrods Food Halls tomorrow. I have an entire list of truffles I need to try."

"And to the National Gallery Thursday," Lexi added. "Remember? Van Gogh's two sunflower paintings are there together for the first time in sixty-five years."

"We have use of a small kitchen in the Culinary, but that doesn't sound like it will be enough for that large an order," Juliette said, trying to be practical. "I think we'd need an industrial mixer and oven."

"You are welcome to use the kitchen at the Wakefield estate," Archie replied. "It's extremely large with all the equipment you'll need. We've catered parties for five hundred people there."

Kylie chewed her pencil eraser. "Chocolate frosting? Or vanilla?"

"I believe Lady Lillianne is partial to Curly Wurly," Archie replied.

"Who exactly is Lady Lillianne?" Sadie asked.

"And more importantly—what the heck is a Curly Wurly?" Delaney added.

"Lady Lillianne is Lord and Lady Wakefield's daughter."

"And a Curly Wurly is a candy bar here in London," Jenna piped up. "I saw someone eating one in the airport. Chocolate-covered caramel in this twisty shape. It kinda looks like a ladder."

"Precisely!" Archie replied. "Which should be perfect for the architectural structure."

This time it was Lexi's turn to raise her hand. "Excuse me, I'm the artist. What architectural structure?" She tore a sheet out of Kylie's notebook, preparing to sketch.

"Ah, yes, sorry. I forgot to mention the display for your cupcakes," Archie apologized. "It's a bit complicated…"

"I have a bad feeling about this," Lexi said nervously.

"You see, her ladyship would like a London Bridge… made out of cupcakes."

Lexi gasped. "As in 'London Bridge is falling down'?"

"Precisely," Archie smiled. "The party is to be held in the North Tower Lounge of the Bridge."

Kylie grabbed Delaney's *Guide Book to London* and started flipping through it for information. "The London Tower Bridge spans the Thames River," she read aloud. "It's a bascule bridge—which is French for the word 'seesaw.'"

Lexi nodded. "As in up and down, since the bottom of the bridge goes up and down." She quickly drew a picture of a bridge opened up and a boat sailing under it on the river. "I could do blue gel icing for the water."

"There are two towers on either side and a huge walkway between them," Kylie continued.

"How huge are we talking?" Sadie asked. "Because my dad's contracting shop is all the way back home in New Fairfield." She turned to Archie. "We're bakers, not builders."

"Hey, you're talking to the Queen of Legos," Jenna volunteered. "My little brothers Ricky and Manny are always building bridges. I got this."

"Are we sure, guys?" Kylie cautioned them. "It sounds like a lot of work."

"It sounds kind of awesome," Lexi replied. "I mean, how often do we get to build a bridge made out of two thousand cupcakes?"

"Whatever you need, I'm at your service," Archie replied. "Flour, sugar, baking tins."

Kylie did some quick math and handed him a sheet of paper. "Let's start with this: five hundred Curly Wurly bars and fifty cans of meringue powder. That should be enough for a five-foot-long display, I think."

Archie scratched his head. "What will you do with all that powder?"

Kylie smiled. "We're going to gum-paste glue you a London Bridge that will knock your socks off!"

Archie stared down at his socks. "Yes, well, it's rather chilly today so I like my socks where they are."

Juliette laughed. "What Kylie means is please tell Lord and Lady Wakefield that we're going to make their daughter a wonderful cupcake bridge for her birthday."

Archie looked relieved. "They'll be very pleased! I'll send a car tomorrow bright and early to take you to the Wakefield estate. It's slightly north of London in the countryside." He handed Juliette his calling card.

"Pip, pip, cheerio!" Delaney said, waving good-bye as Archie strolled out of the hotel.

Rising to the Occasion

A limousine pulled into the driveway of the Convoy at 8 a.m. sharp the next day.

"OMG! Do you think that's the car Archie said he was sending for us?" Delaney gasped.

A driver dressed in a suit and cap got out and walked to the passenger-side door.

"Miss Juliette?" he asked their advisor. "My name is Ralph, and I am at your service."

Juliette looked stunned. "Um, okay…" she said.

"I am here to escort you and your group to Wakefield Manor."

"Whoa," Jenna said, whistling through her teeth. "This car is like a block long!"

The driver held the door open for them. "After you."

Juliette climbed in, followed by the girls. The inside of the car was enormous, with leather seats, a TV, and a mini fridge.

"Anyone want a bottle of water or a soda?" Jenna asked, waving a can in the air.

"I feel like a princess," Lexi said. "Do you suppose this is how all the lords and ladies travel in London?"

Juliette shook her head. "I have no idea. I have a feeling Archie is giving us the royal treatment. She took a bottle of water from Jenna. "But I'm going to sit back and enjoy it!"

In about an hour, the limo pulled up to a large iron gate. The driver hit a button on a remote, and the gate slowly slid open to reveal an enormous redbrick mansion.

"I think we're here," Kylie announced, rolling down the window.

"Let me see! Let me see!" Delaney said, climbing over Kylie to stick her head out the window. "Wow! This place looks like a castle!"

Archie was waiting at the front door to greet them. "I trust your journey was comfortable," he said as Juliette climbed out.

"Comfortable? It was awesome," Sadie piped up. "I've never been in a limo before."

"I'll give you a quick tour, then I'll let you get to your work," Archie said, walking them inside. "Wakefield Manor was built in the early nineteen hundreds. Notice the Scottish Baronial architecture and the Romanesque-inspired arched entranceway…" There were white columns and a huge "sitting room" with gold brocade drapes and antique upholstered furniture.

Kylie stared at the spiral staircase in the middle of the foyer. "Where does that go?" she asked Archie.

"To the dormitories," he explained. "There are a north and south wing, extensive gardens, a small pond, and stables…"

"Stables? As in horses?" Lexi asked. "Oh, that's so cool. I love to draw horses."

"The estate is forty thousand square feet, and His Lordship is particularly proud of the original flora and fauna adornments." Archie pointed to an arch carved with etched images of flowers, grapes, and hummingbirds.

"Wow! Impressive!" Lexi said, getting a closer look.

Next, Archie opened a door to a large room that was lined floor to ceiling with bookshelves. "And this is the library," he said. "I believe there are over four thousand volumes."

Juliette gently took a book off a shelf and looked at the cover. "Is this a first edition of *Peter and Wendy* by J. M. Barrie?" she marveled.

"Yes, Lady Lillianne has always been quite fond of Peter Pan. I believe that was a gift for her last birthday."

"I got a cell phone for my last birthday, and I was totally psyched," Delaney said. "Do you think Lillianne was happy with a book?"

Archie considered. "I should say so. It costs one thousand, two hundred pounds—about two thousand of your dollars."

"A two-thousand-dollar book?" Sadie gasped. "That is crazy. I'd be afraid to turn the pages."

"I dunno," Delaney replied. "I think I'd still rather have a phone than some old, dusty book."

Archie escorted them into the pantry. "This is where you'll find all the supplies you need." He pointed to six large cartons in the corner. "Your Curly Wurly bars, as requested."

Jenna dove for them. "Seriously? Five hundred candy bars? I think I've died and gone to heaven!"

"And through here," he said, leading them into an enormous kitchen, "is where you'll be baking."

Kylie's eyes grew wide. "I've been in big kitchens before, but never anything like this!" she said, admiring not one, not two, but *four* industrial ovens. Every pot and pan was polished to a sparkling finish, and everything was in its proper place. She had never seen a kitchen so neat and tidy. "Now *I* think I've died and gone to heaven."

"His Lordship hosts affairs all the time at the Manor, so

the kitchen was designed to accommodate any food preparation needed. We had a gathering for three hundred just last month."

"Thank you, Archie. It's all incredible," Juliette gushed. "I think we'll just settle in and get started."

Archie nodded. "Of course. I'll leave you to it. Please don't hesitate to summon me." He pointed to a button on an intercom on the wall. "Just ring if you need any assistance."

☆ ☮ ☆

It took the girls nearly an hour to get their bearings and find all the ingredients they needed in the pantry.

"Do you suppose," Delaney wondered out loud, "Lady Lillianne is psyched for her stuffy b-day bash? I mean, don't ya think she'd rather have a bowling party or a sleepover or something?" She was melting milk chocolate in a double boiler on the stove.

"I would be psyched," Lexi said. "If my parents wanted to throw me a fancy party on a bridge, I'd say go for it."

"From the looks of things around here, Lill leads a pretty boring life," Jenna said. "Who arranges their spices in alphabetical order? I mean, come on!"

"I'd like to be nobility," Lexi said, balancing a small

bowl on her head. "I'd love to wear a crown and sit on a throne."

"You'd hate it!" Jenna insisted. "We all would. Part of the fun of baking is making a mess. What if you never could do that?"

Lexi looked down at her T-shirt. It was covered in meringue powder and chocolate smudges. "Yeah, I guess you're right. Still, it would be fun to try it just for a day or so!"

"How are we doing on the salted caramel frosting?" Kylie asked, peeking over Sadie's shoulder. She was mixing butter and dark brown sugar in a saucepan.

"It's bubbling," Sadie said. "I'll give it about two minutes, then let it cool down."

Lexi and Jenna were hard at work using meringue powder to "glue" Curly Wurly bars to the two plywood "towers" Archie had provided for them.

"It's the bridge that's the tricky part," Lexi said, studying the pulley system Jenna had rigged up. At first, they cranked the handle and the rope pulled the bridge up effortlessly—just like the Lego bridge Jenna's brothers had built at home. "It goes up and down just fine when it's the lightweight wood. But add all these candy bars and then the cupcakes…"

"It won't budge." Jenna sighed. "It's just too heavy."

"It needs an elevator," Delaney suggested.

"It needs my dad," Sadie said, sighing. "He would know what to do to fix it."

"We could call him," Delaney suggested. "What time is it back in Connecticut?"

Kylie glanced at her watch. "They're five hours behind us. It's five in the morning in New Fairfield!"

"Forget that idea," Sadie said. "Dad wouldn't appreciate a call at the crack of dawn."

Kylie remembered what her mom had said, how they were all growing up and learning to stand on their own two feet. "We're gonna have to figure it out ourselves," she said. "Think, guys! What could we use to lift the heavy drawbridge up, up, and away?"

"A helium balloon!" Delaney suggested.

"Yeah, that would work," Jenna replied sarcastically. "If the balloon was six feet wide!"

"If pulling won't work, what about pushing?" Kylie pondered. "I remember when my dad got a flat tire a few weeks ago, he used this thing to prop up the whole front of the car."

"A floor jack!" Sadie exclaimed. "Yeah, my dad uses

them all the time to lift stuff that's super heavy. It's got this cool hydraulic system. You just crank the handle down, and it lifts the stuff right up."

"Sounds perfect," Jenna said. "Where do we get one of these floor jacks three thousand miles from home?"

"I'm sure they have them in London," Kylie said. "We'll ask Archie to help us find one. In the meantime, we'll get all the cupcakes baked, decorated, and stuck to the towers and the bridge."

They worked for nearly six hours straight, till every available surface of the Wakefield Manor kitchen—every countertop and shelf, even the seats of chairs—was covered with two thousand mini cupcakes. Lexi rolled out small discs of silver fondant to place on top of each cupcake's frosting. When they covered the sides and tops of the bridge with the cupcakes, it would look like it was made of metal.

While Kylie, Sadie, and Jenna glued each cupcake down, Lexi and Delaney used blue piping gel to make the Thames River around the display.

They stood back and admired their handiwork. It did look pretty amazing!

"It's smashing!" Delaney remarked. "That's British for totally awesome."

Kylie secretly hoped that when they got to Lady Lillianne's party, their tower of cupcakes wouldn't come "smashing" down!

9

A Very Proper Party

As the taxi pulled up to the Tower Bridge on Thursday morning, the girls felt like they were stepping back in time.

"This used to be the only way to cross the Thames River," Delaney read from her guidebook. "It took eight years to build the bridge."

"I'm glad our bridge didn't take that long to build," Kylie said. "We never would have made it in time for the party."

They took the elevator up to the North Tower Lounge and, as soon as they walked in, spotted their cupcake bridge on display on a large table in the center of the room.

"This place is really cool," Sadie said, noticing the gray brick walls and floor-to-ceiling windows. There were dozens of tables already set up and a full waitstaff passing appetizers out from silver platters.

"Don't mind if I do!" Jenna said, sampling a mini crab puff. "*Delicioso!*"

Lexi checked to make sure nothing on their display had come loose or gotten smushed in transport.

"It's perfect," she said, inspecting it. "Not a bit of icing is out of place."

"Just like the Wakefield Manor kitchen." Jenna snickered. "Till we hit it!"

Kylie was crossing her fingers that Archie would come through with the floor jack in time to present their cupcakes to the birthday girl. The guests were set to arrive at 11 a.m. sharp for the festivities—and it was nearly quarter of.

"Where are the streamers and the balloons?" Delaney asked, wandering around the lounge. The only things "decorating" the tables were floral centerpieces and settings of crystal and china. "Do you think they'll have a deejay?"

A string quartet began playing classical music in the corner. "Does that answer your question?" Jenna replied. "Like I said, this is one uppity party."

The guests began arriving right on time, but there was no sign of Archie, Lord or Lady Wakefield, or Lillianne.

"I suppose I could phone Archie," Juliette suggested

as the room filled up with people. The men all wore suits and ties, and the ladies were in dresses with matching coats and fancy hats. "Let's give him a few more minutes," she added, scanning the room. "I'm sure they'll make an entrance soon."

Kylie looked down at her T-shirt. It read, "B UR SELFIE." She and her fellow PLCers stuck out like a single chocolate sprinkle on a perfectly frosted vanilla cupcake.

"At least I wore *royal* blue," Delaney said, tugging on her hoodie.

The quartet suddenly fell quiet, and the violinist cleared his throat. "Announcing Lord and Lady Wakefield and Lady Lillianne." A pair of double doors in the back of the room swung open, and in walked a couple followed by a pale young girl with blond hair pulled back into a tight bun.

Delaney elbowed Kylie. "That's her! That's Lillianne!" she said.

Kylie stared at the girl's face. She didn't seem very happy or excited for her big double-digit birthday. In fact, she looked rather sad.

Archie was trailing behind the family, carrying a large cardboard box in his arms.

"Your jack," he said, handing the box to Juliette. "Our chauffeur had one in the garage. I trust this will do the trick?"

Sadie looked inside. "Yup, that's it," she said. "Let's set it up."

They positioned the jack just under the base of the bridge. "When I give the signal, you *gently* pump the handle up and down," Sadie instructed Kylie. "Not too fast and not too hard. That jack is stronger than it looks."

After an hour of passed appetizers and champagne toasts, it was time to serve dessert. Archie motioned for the quartet to be silent once again. "Ladies and gentleman, may I call your attention to the center of the room where Peace, Love, and Cupcakes has a very special treat for Her Ladyship in honor of her birthday."

Lillianne strolled over to the cupcake display. "Did you make this?" she asked Kylie.

"Um, yeah. We all did. Do you like it?"

The girl walked around the table, taking in the display from every angle.

"Yes," she answered simply.

"Wow, so much for enthusiasm," Jenna muttered under her breath. "Let's get this thing over with."

As everyone gathered around, Sadie gave the cue for Kylie to pump the handle. The quartet began to play "London Bridge Is Falling Down…"

"It's stuck," Kylie whispered to Sadie. "I can't get the handle down."

"Push harder," Sadie instructed her. "Delaney, Lexi, give her a hand."

All three girls grabbed the handle and tried to push it down. The jack wouldn't budge.

"Is it supposed to move?" Lillianne asked with a yawn.

"We're working on it," Kylie said. "Jenna, get in here and help us!"

"On the count of three," Sadie instructed them. "One, two, *three*!"

The handle finally yielded and the jack sprang up, taking the left side of the bridge with it. An entire row of cupcakes flew in the air as if they'd been launched out of a cannon. They landed smack on the birthday girl's perfect white lace party dress.

"Oh, no!" Her mother raced forward to try and rescue her. "Your dress, darling! It's ruined!"

Kylie braced herself for Lillianne to have a total meltdown in the middle of her party. She was completely covered in caramel frosting and chocolate candy. It was a Curly Wurly catastrophe!

"We're so sorry," Kylie apologized to the Wakefields. "We've never used a jack before."

Lady Lillianne didn't cry or scream. Instead, she just smiled from ear to ear.

"This is the best birthday party I've ever had!" she exclaimed, tasting the frosting off her skirt. Her mother was delighted to see her so happy, and the rest of the guests dug into the display, oohing and ahhing about how delicious it all was.

"It's messy but marvelous," the birthday girl's neighbor told Lady Wakefield. "Such good fun!"

Archie was mopping his head with a handkerchief. "I thought we were in serious trouble for a moment," he told Juliette. "But that was the Duchess herself. And if she says it's good fun, then it's good fun."

The person having the most fun of all was Lillianne. She was stuffing her mouth with Curly Wurly bits and smudging frosting on her face.

"I'm never allowed to get messy," she explained. "I love it."

Jenna handed her another cupcake. "It tastes really good

when you eat it like this." She broke off the bottom of the cupcake and put it over the top, smushing it into a "cupcake-wich."

"Brilliant!" Lillianne squealed as the frosting oozed out the sides.

She turned to Kylie. "Can I come bake with you some time? Is it always like this?"

Kylie surveyed the frosting-covered floor, the mess of torpedoed cupcakes, and the guests licking their fingers.

"Yup," she said. "Pretty much an average day for PLC."

10

Opening-Night Jitters

When Rodney called Juliette to check on how everything was going, she barely recognized his voice on the phone.

"I have a touch of laryngitis," he croaked.

"A touch? You sound like a frog!"

After Juliette talked to Rodney, she and the girls raced around London taking in the sights. But Kylie noticed that their advisor was not her usual cheerful self.

"I'm just worried about Rodney," she told them as they perched at the top of the London Eye. The giant glass Ferris wheel offered a stunning view of the entire cityscape. But Juliette barely noticed. "He never gets sick," she said with a sigh.

"My mom always gets a cold whenever she's on a magazine deadline," Kylie told her. "She says it's from the stress."

"I'm sure Rodney's laryngitis is from stress too," Juliette replied. "He's under so much pressure with the play. He wants it to be a huge success, and it's all resting on his shoulders."

"It *will* be a huge success," Kylie assured her. "Mr. Higgins is an amazing actor. The critics are going to love him."

Juliette shrugged. "Not if they can't understand a word he's saying because he's lost his voice. Or worse! What if he can't go on at all?"

Later, as they wandered the rows of stands at the Harrods Food Halls sampling sweets and treats, Jenna suddenly had a brilliant idea.

"You know, when I'm sick, my *abuela* has a home remedy that always works," she mentioned.

"What is it? Maybe we can find it here for Mr. Higgins," Kylie said.

"*Jengibre y canela*," Jenna said. "Ginger and cinnamon."

"We can bring him that," Delaney said.

Kylie smiled. "We can do better. We can *bake* him that."

Juliette overheard their conversation. "It's a lovely idea, girls. But there's no time. Not if you want to get to the London Tombs today and Madame Tussauds. Kylie, I know that was top of your list."

Kylie saw the worry in Juliette's eyes and her decision was easy. "Let's go bake some get-well cupcakes for Mr.

Higgins," she said, pulling her friends with her. "Everything else can wait."

☆ ☮ ☆

It took just over an hour at the kitchen in the Culinary to whip up some cinnamon cupcakes with ginger cream-cheese frosting. Lexi made her "Rain in Spain" fondant designs, and they packaged the cupcakes in a box with a big blue bow.

When they arrived at his flat, they found Rodney wrapped in a blanket. He looked exhausted and pale, and Juliette swooped in the room and led him back to the couch to rest.

"I'll make you some tea," she said, propping his feet up on the pillows. "And the girls can serve you their get-well treats."

Rodney nodded. The doctor had given him strict orders not to speak until the show's opening.

"Do you get what song it's supposed to be?" Lexi said, opening the box to reveal the umbrella, sombrero, and plane modeled out of fondant.

He smiled and gave them a thumbs-up.

"Told ya so!" Lexi said, placing a cupcake on a plate for each of the girls, Mr. Higgins, and Juliette.

"You're going to be okay to go on, right?" Delaney asked. "I mean, you can't miss your own opening night!"

Rodney frowned and shrugged.

"Of course you'll be fine," Juliette said, rubbing his shoulders. "All you need is a little TLC from PLC."

When they said good-bye, Kylie sensed that Juliette didn't want to leave. She held tight to Rodney's hand.

"I feel so bad for Mr. Higgins," Lexi said.

"I feel so bad for Juliette," Kylie replied. "I've never seen her so upset and worried. I wish there was something we could do for her. She does everything for us."

They decided the best game plan was to start working on the *Pygmalion* cupcakes and cross their fingers that Rodney rested up and healed in time for the Sunday-night curtain.

Juliette stayed with them at the Culinary supervising their baking. They tried to take her mind off things by talking about Blakely and what plays they wanted to put on in Juliette's drama class.

"I think we should do *Willy Wonka*," Jenna suggested. "Can you just imagine the set we could build for that? A whole lake made out of chocolate!"

Delaney thought that Lexi would make a great

Oompa-Loompa. "I could paint your face orange for you," she volunteered. "I've done a lot of plays at my school, Weber Day. I'm a pro."

Lexi wrinkled her nose. "Pass—even if you are a pro, no one is painting me to look like a tangerine!"

Kylie wanted to put on Mary Shelley's *Frankenstein* and play the monster himself. She stuck her arms out in front of her and pretended to have a glazed look in her eyes. "You stay. We belong dead!" she muttered.

"Way too creepy for me," Lexi said. "Pass again."

"What play would you like to do, Sadie?" Kylie asked.

"Oh, that's easy. *A League of Their Own*. It was a movie about a team of female ballplayers. Totally up my alley. It would make an amazing play."

Kylie glanced over at Juliette. She was texting Rodney for the third time in an hour.

"So do you think any of these would work for next semester?" she asked her advisor hopefully.

"Huh? Oh, I don't know, Kylie. I can't even think about school right now. I'm too worried about Rodney. Blakely is the furthest thing from my mind."

Kylie looked confused. "What do you mean? We're going back next Monday."

"Yes, we are," Juliette said, sighing. "And that's the problem."

Kylie tried to grasp what Juliette was saying. She remembered the same feeling in the pit of her stomach when her favorite drama teacher, Miss Valentine, left Blakely. It was Juliette who had replaced her, and Juliette who had suggested that Kylie start the cupcake club. "You mean, you don't want to go back to Blakely?"

The words hung in the air, and Juliette didn't argue with them.

"I don't know what I want," her teacher said softly. "But Rodney is here, and I'm there. It doesn't seem right."

She walked out of the kitchen and left the girls to their baking. Kylie tried to shake the thought out of her head. She couldn't imagine PLC without Juliette there to guide them. How could they ever have a cupcake club without her?

Curtains Up!

By Sunday morning, Rodney's voice had improved greatly. His throat was still sore, but he was able to project and not just croak out his lines.

"I think I'll make it," he assured Juliette on the phone. "Are the cupcakes ready? We have a ton of press coming to the opening-night party, and we need to impress them."

Juliette peered out her bedroom door into the living room of their hotel suite. Kylie, Jenna, Lexi, Sadie, and Delaney were all in period costume: long dresses, aprons, shawls, and straw hats.. Each carried two baskets of massive cupcake bouquets.

"Looks like it," she told Rodney. "Thank your friend Marietta in the costume department for lending us the dresses and hats. It's very authentic. I feel like the girls could go peddle their petals in Covent Garden."

Rodney chuckled. "I left you all tickets at the box office. Front row. Don't be late."

Juliette smiled. "I'll be there. Don't you worry."

☆ ☮ ☆

When they arrived at the theater that night, Rodney's name was in huge lights on the marquee. "It gives me goose bumps!" Juliette said, snapping a picture on her phone. "I'm so proud of him."

"We should drop off the baskets of cupcakes backstage," Kylie suggested.

"Ooh! I'll come with you!" Delaney volunteered. "I've always wanted to see what it's like backstage at a real theater."

"Me too," said Sadie. "You guys need extra hands to juggle all those baskets."

Juliette checked her watch. "Fine. Lexi, Jenna, and I will meet you in the seats. Don't take too long."

"Yeah," Lexi warned them. "And be careful with my petal piping."

They made their way down the alley behind the theater and knocked on the stage door. A short, bald man in a vest answered. "Can I help you?" he asked.

"Oh, yes," Kylie replied. "We're here to deliver the cupcakes for the party following the show."

The man looked in their baskets. "I don't see any cupcakes," he said. "Looks like flowers to me."

"Oh, but they are cupcakes!" Kylie said, holding the basket closer to his nose. "Lavender honey cupcakes, to be exact. Have a sniff."

The man took a deep breath. "Smells good. Bet they taste good too."

"They do!" Delaney assured him. "They're delicious."

"Delicious or not, I can't let you back here fifteen minutes before curtain. Those are the rules, ladies."

Kylie smiled sweetly. "But we can't bring all these cupcakes to our seats. They'll get ruined. Pretty please? Couldn't you break the rules just this once?"

The stagehand held out his hand. "You give me one of those cupcakes, and I'll let you inside for five minutes."

Kylie picked a pink rose one out of her basket and gave it to him. "Deal."

The backstage was bustling with activity. There were all sorts of characters in costume, hair and makeup people doing last-minute touch-ups, and a tall man with glasses who was barking orders. "He must be the director," Delaney whispered. "He looks mean."

"Places! Places!" the man shouted. "Take the house to half!" The lights in the theater dimmed.

"Oh my gosh," Sadie said, "We're going to miss the opening scene."

She and Kylie placed their baskets on a table backstage. "Let's go, Laney," Kylie whispered, "Before we get in trouble."

But it was too late. The curtain was rising, the play was starting, and Delaney was making her way with the rest of the flower girls into the Covent Garden set.

"Delaney! No! You're going the wrong way!" Kylie whispered from the wings.

"Kylie, we have to get out of here—now!" Sadie said, pulling her by the arm.

"What about Delaney?" Kylie said. "We can't just leave her."

Sadie looked out onstage. There was Delaney, circling the stage and pretending to sell flowers to the British gentlemen and ladies in the scene. She looked blissfully happy in the spotlights. "I think she's okay. Let's get to our seats before we miss the whole show. Or worse: that director guy figures out we're not supposed to be here."

During a break in the first act, the usher showed them to their seats. Lexi leaned over and grabbed Kylie's arm. "Was that Delaney up there?" she whispered. "We thought we saw her. What's going on?"

"It's a long story," Kylie whispered back. "She kinda took a wrong turn and wound up a flower girl."

"Yeah, a wrong turn on purpose!" Sadie complained. "That girl always likes to be center stage!"

"Look!" Jenna said, shaking her head in disbelief. "There she is again!"

This time, their friend was standing right behind Eliza Doolittle as she defended herself to Henry Higgins. "I never spoke to him except to ask him to buy a flower off me," the actress said. Rodney as Henry Higgins took notes and read them back to Eliza, making fun of the way she talked: "Ow, guv-uh-nuh, tell 'im!" He was hilarious and the audience roared with laughter.

Delaney winked at her friends but stayed in character, listening intently to the scene unfold.

"This is terrible!" Lexi said. "You have to get her out of there."

Juliette chuckled. "I think she's doing a fine job."

Thankfully, during intermission, Delaney snuck out

the backstage door and joined them in the audience. "Oh my gosh! I can't believe I just played the West End." She giggled. "Did you guys see me? I went the wrong way and wound up smack in the middle of the stage! But then I was there and it was so amazing, so I stayed and kinda winged it."

"You winged it very well," Juliette said. "I'm not even sure anyone noticed an extra flower girl in the scene."

"I hope they noticed," Delaney said. "I tried my best!"

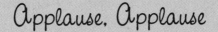
The rest of the play went smoothly—Rodney was an amazing Henry Higgins and his voice held out for the entire show, even the finale when he boomed at Eliza, "By George, I said I'd make a woman of you and I did!"

The audience erupted into thundering applause and gave him a standing ovation. Juliette whistled through her teeth and shouted "Bravo!" as Rodney blew her a kiss from the stage.

At the after-party, everyone congratulated the cast and crew on a job well done. The stage was set up with tables filled with all kinds of delicious treats.

"Prestat Red Velvet Truffles!" Jenna said, spying a platter. "I'm in heaven!"

"What did you think?" Rodney asked, rushing up behind Juliette and planting a kiss on her cheek.

"I thought you were absolutely wonderful," she replied.

"As did I," said a dapper gentleman. "May I shake your hand, sir? Your Professor Higgins was spot-on!"

Rodney blushed. "Thank you. Thank you very much."

"Cupcake, *guh-vuh-nuh*?" Delaney asked, waving the basket under the man's nose.

"Don't mind if I do," he replied, choosing a yellow daisy one. He took a bite. "And these cupcakes are spot-on as well!" He continued to make his way around the stage, mingling with the crowd.

"Do you know who that was?" Rodney said, trying to catch his breath.

"A guy with great taste in theater and cupcakes?" Kylie replied.

"No! I mean, yes!" Rodney stammered. "But he's also the chief theater critic for the *Times*!"

"That means you're gonna get a great review, right?" Delaney asked.

Rodney crossed his fingers. "I think we have a good chance." He turned to Juliette. "Can you believe this is happening?"

Juliette beamed. "No, I can't. It's a dream come true."

Just then the play's director, Nicholas Laughton, found Rodney. "Good show, old boy," he said. "I have a few notes for you, but I think it went very well indeed."

Delaney held up her basket. "Cupcake?" she said, smiling. He reached in and took a white carnation one.

"You! I know you!" Mr. Laughton said, staring at Delaney. "How do I know you?"

Sadie grabbed her friend by the elbow and tried to tug her away. "Um, she has one of those faces," she told the director. "Ya know."

"No, I don't know," he replied. "But you look so familiar..." Before he could get a closer look, Sadie had pulled Delaney out of his sight.

"Phew! That was a close one!" Delaney said. "Thanks, Sadie."

When all the food was gobbled up, it was time for a toast. Rodney clinked a fork on the rim of his champagne flute.

"Pardon me, everyone. If I could please have Archie, as well as my lovely fiancée, by my side? Oh yes. And the girls from Peace, Love, and Cupcakes."

The girls all looked at each other. "What's going on?" Lexi whispered to Kylie. "Did you know about this?"

Kylie shook her head. "Nuh-uh. Maybe he wants to thank us for the cupcakes."

A man dressed in a black robe and white collar came forward, and the orchestra in the pit began to play "Get

Me to the Church on Time" from *My Fair Lady*. Everyone else onstage seemed just as surprised and confused.

"What's going on?" Kylie whispered to Rodney.

"You'll see." He winked.

He took Juliette's hands in his. "There is nothing that would make this night more wonderful than for you to become Mrs. Higgins."

"Oh my gosh!" Lexi squealed. "They're getting married!"

Archie pulled two gold rings out of his pocket. "I think you'll need these," he said, smiling.

"Dearly beloved," the man in the collar began, "we are gathered here tonight to witness the wedding of Juliette Anne Dubois and Rodney Humphrey Higgins."

"Humphrey?" Jenna cackled. "Oh, that's funny!"

"Shhh!" Kylie hushed her. "It's not funny." She wasn't quite sure how she felt about what was taking place. Part of her was thrilled for her advisor; the other part was shocked and worried about what this all meant for PLC.

"May I have the rings?" the minister asked Rodney. "Do you, Rodney Humphrey, take this woman, Juliette Anne, to be your lawfully wedded wife?"

Rodney placed the ring on Juliette's finger and choked back tears. "I do."

"And do you, Juliette Anne, take Rodney Humphrey to be your lawfully wedded husband?"

"I do," Juliette replied, placing the ring on Rodney's finger.

"Then I hereby pronounce you Mr. and Mrs. Higgins. You may kiss the bride!"

Everyone cheered as Juliette and Rodney embraced.

"Surprise!" Juliette told the girls. "You had no idea you were going to be my bridesmaids when you came to London, did you?"

"You weren't acting, right? This was for real?" Delaney asked.

"One hundred percent." Rodney chuckled. "It was all part of the plan."

Jenna, Lexi, Sadie, and Delaney huddled around the happy couple and hugged them. But Kylie couldn't budge from her spot. She was speechless.

The cast and crew all rushed forward to congratulate them. "Excuse me," Juliette told Mr. Laughton as he patted Rodney on the back and kissed her on both cheeks.

She found her way through the crowd to Kylie. "I hope it wasn't too big a shock," Juliette said, taking her aside.

Kylie tried to think of something, anything to say. Finally the words came to her. "I'm really happy for you,

Juliette," she said. "Really and truly. I'm sad for us, but really happy for you."

Juliette squeezed her hand tightly. "Don't be sad, Kylie. I'll stay through the end of the Blakely school year. And I know I'm leaving the club in the best of hands. I don't think anyone could be a better president, leader, or friend than you."

Now it was Kylie's turn to blush. "Really? You think I can handle it?"

"I know you can."

Kylie still felt uncertain. "But who will our new advisor be? How do we know she'll be as good as you?"

"Well, no one could be," Juliette teased. "But I promise whoever it is will be close. I'll make sure you approve."

"I'll miss you, Juliette," Kylie said, hugging her tight. "If it wasn't for you, I would never have started PLC or made these amazing friends or found a place where I belong at Blakely."

"I'll miss you too, more than you know," Juliette replied. "And if it wasn't for you, Kylie, I wouldn't have found a place where I belong either. But now I belong with my husband, here in London."

Kylie nodded. "I know. Are you gonna teach drama here too?"

Juliette thought for a moment. "Maybe. I think I may go back to acting onstage. Mr. Laughton thinks he might have a juicy role for me in his upcoming play next fall."

"That's awesome," Kylie said. "We'll have to come bake cupcakes for your big opening-night party."

Juliette smiled. "I'm counting on it."

Home, Sweet Home

Back in school the next week, Kylie and the rest of PLC fell right back into their routine of studying and baking.

"Did you see this email order?" Lexi said, handing Kylie a printout at their weekly PLC meeting. "It's for a dozen 'Welcome, Herbie' cupcakes."

"What's a Herbie?" Delaney asked.

"I guess it's a guy," Jenna said, scratching her head. "With a really nerdy name."

"Any more deets?" Sadie asked, spinning a basketball on her fingertip.

"Let's see," Kylie said, reading the email. "Cookies and Cream cupcakes with R2-D2 toppers?"

"As in the robot from *Star Wars*?" Lexi said, shaking her head. "Weird."

"Where and when do they want them?" Sadie asked.

"Please don't tell me it's a rush. I have a huge English essay due Wednesday and basketball practice!"

"It says Friday afternoon at four," Kylie continued. "Pickup here in the teachers' lounge. All PLC members should be present to receive payment."

"Okay, doubly weird," Lexi added. "Some teacher named Herbie wants robot cupcakes? And he wants to meet us all in person?"

"I'm sure it's fine," Juliette assured them. "I'll be here to make sure."

Kylie shrugged. "I guess. Whatever. Business is business. We'll bake at Delaney's Thursday night, and her mom can drive her over with the delivery Friday after school."

☆ ☮ ☆

When the girls brought the cupcakes to the lounge Friday, they thought they'd find a Blakely teacher ready and waiting. Instead, the room was empty.

"Uh-oh," Jenna said, looking around. "Do you think we've been stood up?"

"It's just four o'clock," Lexi pointed out. "Juliette isn't even here yet. Let's just take a seat and wait."

The door of the lounge creaked open and Juliette walked

in, accompanied by a tall teenage-looking boy with shaggy brown hair and glasses.

"Ladies, I'd like you to meet Herbie," she said, smiling.

Delaney looked puzzled. "Um, aren't you a little young to be a teacher?"

Herbie hopped up on a stool at the kitchen counter. "I'm actually twenty-three," he said. "I know I look younger than my age."

"You look twelve!" Jenna exclaimed.

"Herbie just graduated from Ontario College," Juliette told them, "With a master's degree in electromechanical engineering."

Now it was Kylie's turn to be confused. "How do you know so much about our client?" she asked her advisor.

Juliette ruffled Herbie's hair. "Because he's my baby brother!"

Kylie's mouth fell wide open. "Your brother? Why didn't you say so? Why the big secret?"

"I'll let Herbie tell you himself," Juliette said, elbowing him in the ribs. "Go on! Tell them!"

"I'm gonna be your new cupcake club advisor," Herbie announced proudly.

"You're what?" Kylie gasped. "I thought you said he has

a degree in electro-whatchamacallit engineering? What do you know about baking cupcakes?"

"Not much," Herbie admitted. "But I'm a fast learner. And FYI, it's electromechanical engineering. I build robots."

"He's going to be Blakely's new robotics teacher," Juliette added. "He's a whiz, really. He'll be able to help you build some amazing cupcake displays."

"Awesome!" Delaney said. "Can you build us a robot that cracks eggs? That's my least favorite part."

"Hey! That's my job!" Sadie protested. "And it's *my* favorite part."

Herbie laughed. "Whatever you want. I'm gonna hang out with you guys for the rest of the semester and get the hang of things. That way, when Juliette moves to London next fall or visits Rodney for a long weekend, we'll be all good."

"All good?" Kylie gulped. "How is a *guy* advising PLC all good?"

Juliette smiled. "I thought you might say that, Kylie. But I did promise you that I would make sure you approved of my replacement."

Herbie unzipped his jacket to show Kylie his T-shirt. It read, "Dr. Frankenstein."

"It's what my friends called me in university," he explained. "I was able to build robots out of bits of this, scraps of that. And I'm a bit of a monster-movie maniac."

Kylie's eyes lit up. "Define 'maniac.' I've seen *The Curse of Frankenstein* twelve times."

"Yeah, well I've seen *Ghost of Frankenstein* twenty-two times," Herbie replied. "I can recite it from memory: 'The lightning! It is good for you!'"

Juliette put one arm around Kylie and the other around her brother. "I do believe you two will get along fabulously," she said. "You always reminded me of my little brother, Kylie."

"Well, at least we can get along when it comes to movies," Kylie said. "I guess we can give you a try with cupcakes too. Speaking of which…"

She handed Herbie a box. "As requested: Cookies and Cream with R2-D2 toppers. Dig in."

Herbie opened the box and grinned. "Wow, you guys are really amazing. That thingamabob on top looks exactly like R2!"

Lexi sniffed. "FYI, it's called fondant. Not a thingamabob."

"Yeah, you've got a lot to learn, dude," Jenna said. "But I like your taste in cupcakes. Oreos are my fave."

Juliette raised a cupcake in the air. "Here's to Peace, Love, and Cupcakes forever!" she said.

And Kylie couldn't argue with that!

Turn the page for three delicious
PLC recipes!

Opening-Night Lavender Honey Cupcakes

Lavender Honey Cupcake

Makes 12 cupcakes

- 1¾ cups all-purpose flour
- 2 teaspoons baking powder
- 1½ teaspoons dried lavender
- ½ teaspoon salt
- ½ cup (1 stick) butter, room temperature
- 1 cup sugar
- ¼ cup honey
- 1 teaspoon vanilla extract
- 2 eggs
- ⅔ cup milk

Directions

1. Preheat oven to 350°F. Line muffin pans with cupcake wrappers.

2. Combine flour, baking powder, lavender, and salt in a medium bowl.

3. In a mixing bowl, beat the butter on high for about a minute. Add sugar, honey, and vanilla, then the eggs, one at a time, beating until they are combined. Add in the flour mixture and milk, alternating. Beat about three to four minutes until the batter is smooth (but don't overbeat!).

4. Fill each cupcake wrapper two-thirds full and place in oven. Bake for approximately eighteen to twenty-two minutes, or until a toothpick inserted in the center comes out clean. Allow to cool for fifteen minutes before frosting.

Vanilla Cream Cheese Frosting

12 ounces (one package and a half) cream cheese, room
temperature

½ cup (1 stick) unsalted butter, room temperature

2 teaspoons vanilla extract

4 cups confectioners' sugar

Directions

1. In the bowl of an electric mixer, beat the cream
cheese, butter, and vanilla extract until smooth.
Add the powdered sugar, one cup at a time, and
beat until frosting is creamy and smooth. Pipe onto
cupcakes or apply with a frosting knife or spatula.
If you want to get fancy, add food coloring to the
frosting and pipe it to look like flower petals!

Lady Lillianne's Chocolate Cupcakes with Salted Caramel Frosting

Chocolate Cupcake

Makes 12 cupcakes

- 1½ cups all-purpose flour
- ¾ cup unsweetened cocoa powder
- 2 teaspoons baking powder
- ½ teaspoon baking soda
- 1/8 teaspoon salt
- 3 tablespoons butter, room temperature
- 1½ cups sugar
- 2 eggs
- 1 teaspoon vanilla extract
- ¾ cup milk

Directions

1. Preheat oven to 350°F. Line muffin pan with cupcake wrappers. In a medium bowl, sift together the

flour, cocoa powder, baking powder, baking soda, and salt.

2. In the large bowl of a mixer, cream together the butter and sugar until light and fluffy. Add in the eggs, one at a time, then the vanilla.

3. Add the flour mixture and milk, alternating between them. Beat three to four minutes until the batter is smooth.

4. Fill each cupcake wrapper two-thirds full with batter, and bake in oven for eighteen to twenty-two minutes, or until a toothpick inserted in the center comes out clean. Remove from oven and allow to cool for approximately fifteen minutes before frosting.

Salted Caramel Frosting

1 stick (half cup) salted butter

2 cups dark brown sugar

⅔ cup heavy cream

¼ teaspoon salt

3 cups confectioners' sugar

Directions

1. Ask an adult to help you melt the butter in a small

saucepan over a low flame, stirring constantly. Once the butter is entirely melted, add brown sugar and heavy cream. Stir constantly over medium heat until sugar is dissolved. Add salt. Allow mixture to bubble for exactly two minutes. Remove from heat and allow to cool. Beat in confectioners' sugar, one cup at a time, until the frosting is smooth and creamy.

Lexi's Rainbow Tie-Dye Cupcakes

Rainbow Tie-Dye Cupcake

Makes 18 cupcakes

This recipe calls for a basic vanilla cupcake batter.

3 cups all-purpose flour

1½ teaspoons baking powder

¾ teaspoon salt

12 tablespoons (1½ sticks) unsalted butter, room temperature

1½ cups sugar

4 eggs

2 teaspoons vanilla extract

1¼ cups milk

Box of assorted food coloring

1. Preheat oven to 350°F and line muffin pan with cupcake wrappers. In a medium bowl, sift together the flour, baking powder, and salt.

2. In the large bowl of a mixer, cream together the butter and sugar until light and fluffy. Scrape down the sides.

3. Add eggs one at a time, then the vanilla. Beat until combined.

4. Add the flour mixture and milk, alternating between them. Beat for about three to four minutes, but be careful not to overbeat!

5. Now that you've prepared the batter, it's time to color it! Pour the batter from the large bowl into five smaller bowls. Use two to three drops of food coloring in each bowl to create a bright color. Stir batter in each bowl until it is one color. I like to do red, yellow, orange, blue, and green, but feel free to mix your own shades.

6. Using a tablespoon to scoop out your batter, layer the different colors into each cupcake wrapper until it is two-thirds full. You can use a toothpick to lightly swirl the colors around.

7. Bake for eighteen to twenty-two minutes, or until a toothpick inserted in the center comes out clean. Allow to cool for approximately fifteen minutes before frosting.

8. Feel free to frost your masterpieces with any flavor icing you like!

Carrie's Q and A:
Tarek Malouf, founder of
London's Hummingbird Bakery

When I was in London I *had* to try Hummingbird Bakery! I had heard amazing things about their "American style" cupcakes, and I love their cookbooks! So I went to their shop in Soho and I wasn't disappointed. There were a lot of fun flavors to choose from, everything from Carrot, Red Velvet, and Chocolate Malt (with malt-ball crumbles on top), to my personal fave, Black Bottom. The cake is rich and chocolatey, and in the center is a delicious surprise: cheesecake! The frosting is cream cheese too, and it's topped with chocolate cake crumbs. In a word: *yum*!

Since *Royal Icing* was inspired by my London trip, I asked Hummingbird Bakery's founder Tarek Malouf to answer some questions. He's sold *millions* of cupcakes in his stores, so I figured he was the perfect London cupcake expert to ask!

Carrie: When and why did you decide to open Hummingbird Bakery in the United Kingdom?

Tarek: I opened the first bakery on Portobello Road in Notting Hill in 2004, but the decision to open an American-style bakery was a while in the making. The idea of setting up a bakery came to me in early 2002. I was visiting my aunt in North Carolina, and she took me to several traditional American bakeries that served pies and homemade cakes. The smell of fresh baking in these places was amazing. During that time, my sister was living in New York, and we used to go and eat lots of cupcakes and traditional American goodies every time I'd visit her. Taste buds awakened, it was then that I realized I wanted to open my own bakery in London.

Carrie: How did you come up with the name?

Tarek: The hummingbird is native to the Americas, and it feasts on the sweet nectar of flowers. This image of a beautiful bird with a love of sweet things just seemed to fit the bakery I wanted to create.

Carrie: How many bakeries do you have now? I heard you're in Dubai!

Tarek: We have six bakeries in London located in Notting

Hill, South Kensington, Soho, Spitalfields, Islington, and Richmond. In addition to this, we have an international franchise with two (very soon to be three) stores open in Dubai.

Carrie: What is the difference between a cupcake in the United States and a cupcake in the UK?

Tarek: Well, the cupcakes we bake at the Hummingbird Bakery should be very familiar to anyone from the United States! Moist cake with a generous amount of frosting. Other cupcakes in the UK tend to be a bit smaller, with a thicker, pastier icing instead of buttercream or cream cheese frosting. That's why ours at Hummingbird have been received so well!

Carrie: I think my favorite flavor at Hummingbird was the Black Bottom or the Salted Caramel. What's yours?

Tarek: I have to say, although we're probably best known for our Red Velvet, I also love the Black Bottom cupcake the most! For anyone who hasn't tried it, this is a rich chocolate sponge with a spoonful of chocolate-chip cheesecake baked into it, topped with cream cheese frosting.

Carrie: What are your most popular cupcakes?

Tarek: Red Velvet cupcakes are our bestsellers, followed closely by Black Bottom cupcakes.

Carrie: What are some of the most *unique* cupcakes Hummingbird Bakery has created? Who comes up with the ideas?

Tarek: We are lucky enough to have a product development team that experiments with sponges and frostings to create the cupcakes that eventually reach our counters. We always try to bake cupcakes that we know our customers will love, so we haven't made too many crazy flavors, but, that said, we have created themed cupcake collections that take their inspiration from things as diverse as hot drinks (Earl Grey Tea cupcakes) and a carnival (Popcorn cupcakes). Sometimes the decoration will be what makes our cupcakes really stand out. I particularly loved the range of Milkshake cupcakes that we created. All of them had little red-and-white-striped edible bendy straws.

Carrie: Cool! What makes a *perfect* cupcake, in your opinion?

Tarek: The perfect cupcake has to be freshly baked. For me, there is no competition with a cupcake that is freshly baked and frosted on the same day. All our cupcakes are baked fresh on-site at each of our bakeries on the day. This way, the sponges stay lovely and moist, and the frosting is freshly whipped and deliciously smooth. Also, all our cupcake sponges are completely covered in frosting so that the sponge doesn't dry out.

Carrie: Have you been to the States and sampled any cupcakes here?

Tarek: I visit the States very often and have been doing so since I was two years old. I have a lot of family there and I have a very sweet tooth, so they all know that when I visit, they need to take me to check out the best desserts! My last visit to the United States was part of my preparations for the fourth cookbook we have coming out to follow *Home Sweet Home*. It will gather together some of my favorite all-American baking recipes, so obviously I needed a few taste tests while I was there.

Carrie: Do you think you'll ever bring Hummingbird Bakery to the United States (pretty please!)?

Tarek: Maybe one day. We are currently working hard on our international franchising project and continue to search for suitable locations in the UK and abroad. When I opened my first bakery a decade ago, I never anticipated the demand that would come from overseas for our cupcakes and desserts, but if there's a market for them, we'll do our best to meet that need.

Carrie: How many cookbooks have you written? What is the most recent one?

Tarek: We have three cookbooks that have all hit the best-sellers' lists: *The Hummingbird Bakery Cookbook* (2009, Ryland Peters & Small), *Cake Days* (2011, Collins) and *Home Sweet Home* (2013, Collins). We have a fourth one in the making, which is due out in 2015.

Carrie: How did you get your start in baking? Did you like to bake as a kid? Did you attend culinary school?

Tarek: I'm not a professional baker myself, but I am a very enthusiastic taster of baked goods! I did make stuff for bake sales at school, but I definitely prefer eating cupcakes and sweet goodies. I guess it's cleaning up the mess in the kitchen that puts me off baking too often at home! I did my fair share of baking along the way in the first couple years of opening my business.

Carrie: What is your advice for a kid who wants to grow up and open his or her own bakery?

Tarek: A clear idea of what you want to achieve is crucial to success. Baking is a very competitive industry, so you really have to know  what sets you apart and not lose sight of this vision. And start small! Selling yummy things from a stall or farmers' market is easier and probably more fun at first than the hassle of setting up a real shop. Let things grow organically and slowly.

Acknowledgments

Many thanks to everyone who has embraced The Cupcake Club book series, including in its new form—as an Off-Broadway musical! We love our fans and audiences! Rick Hip-Flores: you are a genius. Broadway beckons!

To the Kahns, Berks, and Saps: as always, thank you for your love and support!

To our friends, new and old, you make life so sweet! Trevor girls rock!

Holly/Maggie: we love that you read our book before it ever hits shelves! XO

A special shout-out to Derry Wilkens, who we will miss dearly at Sourcebooks. What will we do without our whiz of a publicist? Steve, Jillian, Kate, Alex, and the whole gang: thank you for making the process so easy and fun. Katherine Latshaw/Frank Weimann and the Folio group: thanks for taking such good care of our beloved book series and us.

Coming Next Year...

FASHION
ACADEMY

CHAPTER 1

The trip over the Brooklyn Bridge to the Fashion Academy of Brooklyn—aka FAB—had taken longer than she expected, but Mickey Williams didn't mind the bumper-to-bumper traffic or the honking horns. She was taking it all in: the sights and sounds that were New York City, fashion capital of the world! As the kids filed off the school bus, she was able to get a better look at what they were all wearing. She saw several Abercrombie hoodies, a few Brandy Melville graphic tees, and countless pairs of Superga sneakers in boring tennis white.

What happened to pushing the envelope? she wondered. Where was the creativity? The originality? They all looked like carbon copies of each other. FAB was supposed to be cutting edge; a place where the fashion designers of the future went to school! She had convinced her mom there was nowhere else in the world she wanted to go, even if it meant leaving her home in Philadelphia and living with her Aunt Olive in a cramped Upper West Side apartment.

Mickey walked up the steps to the school's huge gray concrete and glass doors. Even the building looked boring.

A voice behind her read her mind. "You were expecting something a bit more artsy, right?"

She turned to see a short boy carrying a tote bag that was almost as big as he was.

"I guess," Mickey replied. "I'm not sure what I was expecting."

"You're new," he said, climbing the steps. "Sixth-grader?"

Mickey nodded. "You?"

"Seventh. I'm Javen Cumberbatch." He dug in the pocket of his jeans and pulled out a business card. Mickey read it: "JC Canine Couture."

"You design for dogs?" she gasped.

The boy raised an eyebrow. "I wouldn't be so judgy, Miss 'I colored my hair with chalk to look like a salad.'"

"It's green, okay? I like green."

He chuckled. "Apparently. I can tell from the splatter paint on your shirt and pants. But your bag rocks. Really." Mickey had stitched together two flannel dust bags used to protect designer purses—one that read PRADA, the other Louis Vuitton—and attached two belts for handles. Total cost from her thrift store scavenger hunt: $4.

Mickey smiled and noticed that JC's bag was moving. "Is there something in there?" she whispered.

He unzipped the top of his tote and a tiny wet nose poked out. "Madonna the Chihuahua, meet…what's your name again?"

"Mickey. Mickey Williams."

"Don't tell anyone, okay?" he said, zipping Madonna back into her home. "No dogs on FAB property. Mr. Kaye would have a fit. But she's kind of my mascot. She goes where I go."

"I promise. Your secret is safe with me," Mickey replied. "But who's Mr. Kaye?"

"Only the toughest Apparel Arts teacher in the entire school."

"Oh," Mickey gulped.

"You definitely want to watch out for him…and those two." He motioned to the curb where a large black stretch limo was pulling up. A girl and a boy stepped out, waving to the crowd of students as if they were royalty.

Mickey wrinkled her nose. "Who are they?"

"The Lee Twins. They're in my grade. Their mom is Bridget Lee, wedding designer to the stars."

Mickey whistled through her teeth. "Whoa! She's super-famous."

"Exacterooni," JC replied. "So steer clear of Blake and Jake. Or as I prefer to call them, Tweedle Mean and Meaner."

Mickey stared at the pair. They looked fairly normal, if not a bit fancy for the first day of school. Blake was wearing white lace shorts and a white chiffon halter top. Her long black hair was pulled back in a rhinestone headband that looked like a tiara. Jake was dressed in a white linen suit with a baby blue polo shirt underneath.

When Blake was done air-kissing all her friends on both cheeks, she took her pink, crushed velvet Chanel backpack from the limo driver and slung it over one shoulder.

"Wow. That bag's not even available yet. It's in the Spring collection," Mickey remarked.

"You know your runway—that's a plus," the boy told her before rushing off to his first class. "Good luck on your first day, Green Girl."

* * *

Mickey tried to decipher her schedule and find her way around FAB's long and winding hallways. There were six floors with design studios on each. In the basement was the FAB auditorium, complete with a real runway worthy of New York or Paris Fashion Week.

Besides the basic middle school classes—math, science, English, and a foreign language—there were two design classes every day.

"Is this Studio 6B? Apparel Arts?" she asked, panting from the climb up all those flights.

A dapper-looking gentleman with graying hair, a mustache, and a plaid bow tie peered at her over the tops of his wire-rimmed spectacles. "And you might be?"

"Lost. I'm lost. I went to two other studios on this floor and they told me I was in the wrong place."

The man tapped his mechanical pencil against his chin. "You don't say? Well, then congratulations. You've come to the right place. Take a seat."

He pointed to a drafting table a few feet from his desk. Mickey looked around the room and noticed the rest of the class was whispering and giggling.

"Is there a problem?" the teacher asked.

"No, no problem," Mickey said, sliding into her seat. She could feel the eyes on the back of her neck.

"Good. Then we can begin. I am Mr. Kaye and this is Apparel Arts 1. Everyone in this class is either new to FAB—or flunked my class last semester." He stared in disapproval at the boy sitting in the desk next to Mickey.

Mickey gulped. This was the teacher JC had warned her about, and she'd already made a bad first impression.

"Every week, you will sketch, design, and create a design based on a theme I assign you," Mr. Kaye began. "At the end of the semester, you will present a ten-piece collection on the runway before a panel consisting of myself, my fellow teachers, and special celebrity guests."

He stood up in front of the SMART Board and drew a big number "1" on it. "Your first challenge will be due in class tomorrow. I will be judging along with your peers."

Mickey's hand shot up. "Excuse me. Peers? We get to judge each other?"

The boy next to her groaned. "No, the winner of the FAB Spring Fashion Show gets to judge the first challenge of the semester. Duh."

Mickey looked confused.

"Blake Lee," the boy whispered. "Get a clue, will ya?"

Mr. Kaye continued. "The theme is World Hunger Day. I would like you to design an original T-shirt that encompasses the theme while demonstrating creativity and originality. I don't want to see something I've already seen before. Any questions?"

Mickey's hand went up again. "Can we use whatever materials we want?" she asked.

"As long as you stick to the budget: no more than ten dollars for the entire design, top to bottom."

A girl in the back row held up a scrap of fabric. "That's impossible. I want to use lavender cashmere silk, and that's way more than ten dollars a yard."

"And we only have till tomorrow?" another boy protested. "Seriously? I'm gonna be up all night sewing!"

"Work it out," Mr. Kaye said with a dismissive wave of his hand. "Work it out."

"Whenever he says that, you know you're in trouble," the boy next to Mickey whispered. "That's what he said right before he gave me a big fat F on my final."

"You may sketch for the remainder of the period," their teacher added. "In silence."

When Mickey got home from school she knew exactly what she needed to do—and she had to work fast on her

Apparel Arts homework assignment before Aunt Olive got home from her job and started asking questions.

She rummaged through the fridge and cupboard shelves and started putting things out on the kitchen table: dried cranberries, beets, carrots, raspberries, blueberries, and pistachio nuts. Her World Hunger Day T-shirt would be entirely decorated with actual food! For the first time she was grateful that her aunt was a vegetarian with a wide array of colored fruits and veggies to choose from. She took a basic white tee and laid it inside a large bowl. Then she began crushing the beets and berries till it was streaked with purple, red, and blue smudges. She used a needle to pierce the cranberries and secure them with thread to the neckline of the shirt. Finally, she used a hot glue gun to adhere the pistachio nuts to the cuffs of the arms.

She stood back and admired her handiwork. It still needed something. But what? She opened the fridge again and spied the perfect thing: a huge head of red cabbage. She quickly stripped off the leaves and sewed them to the hem of the shirt. From a distance, they looked like purple and white ruffles.

Just then, she heard Aunt Olive's key in the door. She

quickly swept all the leftover food and mashed berries into the garbage and tried to wipe the red stains off the countertop.

"Mackenzie? Are you home?" her aunt called.

"Um, I'm in the kitchen. Be out in a sec!" she folded the T-shirt and quickly tucked it into a plastic freezer bag which she tossed into her backpack.

"Oh, good," Olive said, walking to the sink to wash her hands. "You can help me sauté the red cabbage for dinner."

Mickey gulped. "The red cabbage?"

Olive opened the fridge and searched. "Yes, I was sure I put it right here on the third shelf."

Mickey thought quick. "Oh, *that* red cabbage. I'm so sorry, Aunt Olive. I ate it for my afterschool snack."

Olive stared. "You ate an entire head of red cabbage? Raw?"

"Yeah, it was really yummy. I couldn't help myself."

"Well," Olive replied, wiping her hands on her apron. "I'll just have to run out to the grocery and get another. And if you like it so much, I'll get you one for tomorrow as well."

Mickey breathed a huge sigh of relief. "Oh, that would be great. Thanks."

She waited till she heard the door slam to call her mom back in Philadelphia.

"How was your first day, Mickey Mouse?" her mom was dying to know.

"It was good, just different," Mickey explained. "I'm really excited for my Apparel Arts assignment that's due tomorrow. I think I rocked it."

"Of course you did," her mom replied. "I would expect nothing less. Did you make friends?"

"Um, yeah, a couple. This boy JC is nice."

"Is Aunt Olive driving you up the wall yet?" her mom pushed. "Is she making you eat kale milkshakes for breakfast?"

"She just went out to get us some dinner," Mickey said. "Don't worry. I'm fine."

She heard a client in the background asking her mom something about waterproof mascara. "Gotta run, Mouse! Call ya later!"

Convincing her mom FAB was fab was one thing; convincing her best friend was another.

"Are the girls stuck up?" Annabelle wanted to know when Mickey called her next. "I bet they are, right?"

Mickey told her all about Blake and Jake's grand entrance and how JC carried his Chihuahua to classes.

"These kids sound really weird," Annabelle said. "I got my schedule today and it's awesome. I have Dance for first Arts Rotation!"

"Cool," Mickey said, trying to sound excited for her friend. If she had stayed in Philly, they would have been walking to school together every day.

"Oh! And my mom took Rachel Solomon and me for froyo after school! They've got this awesome new flavor that tastes exactly like chocolate milk!"

Mickey missed Annabelle. And froyo. And chocolate milk. "So you and Rachel are now besties?" she asked, fingering the silver scissor charm around her neck. "I thought you hated her because she made fun of your braces last year?"

"Nah, she's okay. We share a locker and she's in my Spanish and math classes."

Mickey nodded. "Sounds cool."

"Well, I gotta run, Mick. I have tons of homework!" She hung up before Mickey could say good-bye.

Olive walked back into the apartment and placed two red cabbages on the kitchen table. "I had to hike all the way to Amsterdam to get organic ones," she said, out of breath from climbing the stairs. Then she noticed Mickey's long face.

"What's wrong with you?"

"Nothing. My best friend just seems really busy."

Olive handed her a pot to put the cabbage in. "You know what they say, 'Out of sight, out of mind,'" her aunt reminded her. "People have to get on with their lives whether or not you're there. It was your decision to go to middle school in New York City."

She knew that was true. She didn't expect her mom to stop working, or Annabelle to stop going to their favorite froyo place. But she also didn't expect to miss them so much.

"How was your first day?" Olive asked. "Everything you thought it would be?"

Mickey didn't feel like fibbing anymore. "It was hard. I couldn't find my classes, and the kids thought I was weird and kind of ignored me." She waited for her aunt to say something, anything, to make her feel better.

Olive pursed her lips. "I'm not sure I'm the best person to give you advice, Mackenzie. I've never been a mother, and I don't have very many friends."

Well, that was true…

"But I do know that most birds will eventually find a flock to fly with. Give it time."

About the Authors

Photo credit: Emily Saperstone

Sheryl Berk is the *New York Times* bestselling coauthor of *Soul Surfer*. An entertainment editor and journalist, she has written dozens of books with celebrities including Britney Spears, Jenna Ushkowitz, and Zendaya. Her daughter, Carrie Berk, is a renowned cupcake connoisseur and blogger (www.facebook.com/PLCCupcakeClub; www.carriescupakecritique.shutterfly.com) with over 101K followers at the tender young age of eleven! Carrie cooked up the idea for the Cupcake Club series while in second grade. To date, they have written six books together (with many more in the works!). *Peace, Love, and Cupcakes* had its world premiere as a delicious new musical at New York City's Vital Theatre in 2014. The Berk ladies are also hard at work on a new series, Fashion Academy, due out on shelves Spring 2015. Stay tuned!

Peace and Love and CUPCAKES

Meet Kylie Carson.

She's a fourth grader with a big problem. How will she make friends at her new school? Should she tell her classmates she loves monster movies? Forget it. Play the part of a turnip in the school play? Disaster! Then Kylie comes up with a delicious idea: What if she starts a cupcake club?

Soon Kylie's club is spinning out tasty treats with the help of her fellow bakers and new friends. But when Meredith tries to sabotage the girls' big cupcake party, will it be the end of the cupcake club?

Book 1

Recipe For Trouble

$\mathcal{M}$eet Lexi Poole.

To Lexi, a new school year means back to baking with her BFFs in the cupcake club. But the club president, Kylie, is mixing things up by inviting new members. And Lexi is in for a not-so-sweet surprise when she is cast in the school's production of *Romeo and Juliet*. If only she could be as confident onstage as she is in the kitchen. The icing on the cake: her secret crush is playing Romeo. Sounds like a recipe for trouble!

Can the girls' friendship stand the heat, or will the cupcake club go up in smoke?

Book

2

Winner Bakes All

$\mathcal{M}$eet Sadie.

When she's not mixing it up on the basketball court, she's mixing the perfect batter with her friends in the cupcake club. Sadie's definitely no stranger to competition, but the oven mitts are off when the club is chosen to appear on *Battle of the Bakers*, the ultimate cupcake competition on TV. If the girls want a taste of sweet victory, they'll have to beat the very best bakers. But the real battle happens off camera when the club's baking business starts losing money. Long recipe short, no money for icing and sprinkles means no cupcake club.

With the clock ticking and the cameras rolling, will the club and their cupcakes rise to the occasion?

Book
3

Icing on the Cake

Meet Jenna.

She's the cupcake club's official taste tester, but the past few weeks have not been so sweet. Her mom just got engaged to Leo—who Jenna is sure is not "The One"—and Peace, Love, and Cupcakes has to bake the wedding cake. Jenna is ready to throw in the towel, especially when she hears the wedding will be in Las Vegas on Easter weekend, one of the most important holidays for the club's business!

Can Jenna and her friends handle their busy orders—and the Elvis impersonators—or will they have a cupcake meltdown?

Book
4

Baby Cakes

$\mathcal{M}$eet Delaney.

New cupcake club member Delaney is shocked to find out her mom is expecting twins! When her parents first tell her, the practical joker thinks they must be pulling her leg. For ten years she's had her parents—and her room—all to herself. She LIKED being an only child. But now she's going to be a big sis.

The girls of Peace, Love, and Cupcakes get together to bake cupcakes and discover Delaney is worried about what kind of a big sister she will be. She's never even babysat before! But her cupcake club friends rally to her side for a crash course in Baby Sister 101.

Book

5